Betra

M A Macklin

Chapter 1

St Wilfrid's Academy

Since their first day at primary school, Rupert Gilby and Daniel Dawson had been good friends. Both boys were shy, artistic and above average intelligence. They decided their lives would be easier if they could blend into the background at the far end of the playground, far away from all the rough and tumble and of course, any would-be bullies…

Rupert's father was a stock-broker: a successful man who'd become accustomed to getting his own way. Despite numerous heated rows with his wife, stony silences and days with nothing more tempting than a ready-prepared salad thrust under his nose, Hugo Gilby refused to change his mind. His sons, Rupert and Piers, would *not* be attending St Wilfrid's Academy in Chichester. Barrington Road comprehensive, in Eastbourne, would be more than capable of preparing his boys for the real world…

Besides, school fees of £10,000 per term, for each boy, would be crippling.

Hugo knew they would never agree on the matter, so, perhaps he should try a little bribery. Alicia's wardrobe was fit to bursting, but a surprise cash injection into her personal bank account usually worked wonders. Hugo was fed up with cold meals and besides, the spare bedroom was not where he wanted to be…

Eventually, he managed to persuade his wife that a vast amount of money like this would be better spent on luxury cars or holidays in the Seychelles; something to impress her snooty and equally wealthy friends.

Hugo had endured seven years at St Wilfrid's Academy and loathed every moment; his sons would not be following in the family tradition. Hours of Latin and Greek? Not for his boys. He shivered; memories came flooding back. A weekly four-mile cross-country run, regardless of the weather, then, cold showers! *No, never.*

The very thought of coming face to face with the sickly grin and lengthy cane belonging to the headmaster, Mr Bartlett, had reduced some of the boys to a quivering wreck. The aging Bartlett had lived with Mr Hardwick, the games master, for nearly twenty years. If anxious parents asked too many probing questions (they did, back in the 1960s) they were reassured by the school's governing body – the headmaster and the games master were no more than 'second cousins.'

Mr Hardwick was a man with an unhealthy and disturbing pastime...

After the boys had taken part in a lively game of rugby or other outdoor activity, Hardwick, in his early forties, could be seen parading up and down – gazing into the shower cubicles, just as the boys were stripping off. Rumours spread amongst the boys – Hardwick too must be given a very wide berth...

Hugo shook his head, trying to erase memories of the sadistic canings handed out by both masters. Corporal punishment had been declared illegal in the 1980s and things had improved, but slowly.

Sometimes, even now, Hugo was plagued by a recurring nightmare: he was sitting outside the headmaster's study, shaking, waiting to be called inside over some minor misdemeanour…

Claude Bartlett died from lung cancer, aged sixty-seven. Wishing to start a new life (and much to everyone's surprise) Reggie Hardwick sold the charming bungalow he'd shared with Claude and moved to Ibiza. Six months later, according to the Eastbourne Gazette, Reggie was robbed then murdered, outside a sleezy nightclub, his battered body dumped by the side of the road.

Hugo and Alicia were delighted; their youngest son had palled-up with a sensible, well-mannered and likable boy. Yes, Daniel Dawson, although from a working-class background, would be an excellent influence on Rupert.

Aged eighteen, Rupert and Daniel left Eastbourne, an exciting future beckoned, three years studying at the University of East Anglia, with several trips to Europe, including Florence and Venice. These were the good times when study and socializing competed for their attention. Both young men left Norwich with a first-class honour's degree in the History of Art.

It was later, back home in Sussex, when their friendship came under scrutiny; life would be sending them down different paths. It was easy for Hugo to point his sons in the right direction; he had friends at Westminster (in the Commons and the Lords) plus several old school chums in the City.

Daniel decided to take a year off before beginning the arduous task of job-hunting. He enjoyed working part-time in his dad's corner shop, especially meeting and befriending the customers.

Studying art in all its many forms, had been a wonderful choice, but finding a career within its closed and snobbish ranks would be easier said than done…

Sanderson's Art Gallery was based in the town centre and run by Janice, a friend of his mother. When Danny received an enthusiastic reply to his short email, he was delighted – such kindly words too. Would he consider working part-time, especially weekends and during the school holidays? His knowledge and warm personality would give the gallery such a lift!

Two jobs, thought Daniel, but neither will be challenging and the money will go towards my first car.

Danny ripped open the long blue envelope: what a surprise, an invitation (embossed in gold lettering) to Rupert Gilby's belated twenty-first birthday bash, to be held in London, at the Excelsior Gentleman's Club. Rupert's father, and his father before him, had been lifelong members. Rupert wanted to wait until his university days were over before having a *wild* party! As his parents were picking up the bill, he hadn't objected when they insisted on choosing the venue…

Danny frowned. Oh, heck, was posh stuff required, like white tie and tails? He hurried across the worn-out bedroom carpet and opened his wardrobe door. Who am I kidding? He shook his head. I've only got jeans, a couple of checky shirts plus loads of sweatshirts and T shirts. At least I've got a pair of smart black shoes and I suppose I could borrow dad's best white shirt…

He felt nervous, surely, he'd feel out of his depth? Much easier to say thanks, but no, he had a prior engagement on the 15th.

Jenny Dawson smiled at her son, "Don't be so daft, of course you must go, he's your best friend. I've got an idea. Cyril Watts, down the road – he goes to lots of civic functions, he'll know the dress code. Do you remember, he was Mayor of Eastbourne three years ago? He'll lend you a suit and tie: he's a bit shorter than you and rather tubby but we can make it fit. I'll give him a ring in the morning."

"Oh, mum, I look absolutely ridiculous, like a clown, the trousers are too short and there's so much spare cloth around the waist, *you could fit another me inside!* Even if I wear a belt, they still won't hang right."

Jenny laughed. "Oh, don't make such a fuss, you're exaggerating. They'll be fine once you put the jacket on. You're as good as any of them – better than most!"

Encouraged by his mother's soothing words, Danny set off for London, catching the six-fifteen train to Victoria station.

The moment Danny entered the vast dining room he knew he'd made a terrible mistake; he didn't recognise anyone! Hoots of laughter rang out. Why is it, he thought, people like this make me feel so small, so uncomfortable?

Why are they staring in my direction? Then the penny dropped: they were laughing at *him!*

He'd over-tightened the belt on his trousers and now, after walking from the station, one trouser-leg had ridden-up, looking shorter than the other and a faded, crumpled grey sock was showing. To make matters worse, a pigeon had pooped on him, just above his left shoulder-blade. One of the 'Hooray Henrys' (who'd already consumed a vast amount of champagne) spotted the filthy greyish-white stain, pointed to it, then fell about in hysterics…

Another young man, with bright ginger hair, started throwing mini sausage rolls in Danny's direction, the final one clipping his right ear. *"Come on guys,"* he shouted, *"let's get the bastard! He's not one of us!"*

Suddenly, the room seemed to be closing in on him. Danny turned and ran down the narrow corridor and out into the damp night, still clutching Rupert's birthday presents.

The box of chocolates and a pair of tan leather gloves – both from Harrods, were handed to the first rough sleeper he could find. The poor chap, the wrong side of sixty, gave a toothless grin, ripped open the box of chocolates and winked in Danny's direction. No doubt, living on London's soul-less streets, he'd experienced far stranger things.

The following morning, over tea and toast, Danny's mum questioned him about the party.

"Yeah, I had a fantastic time. I caught up with some old friends, we had a blast."

"Sorry we didn't wait up, love, but we'd no idea what time you'd get home. Any pretty girls there?"

Danny chuckled. "You bet. As usual, I was fighting them off…"

How could he tell his mother what really happened? Utter humiliation. It'd been the worst night of his life.

After escaping from the Excelsior Club, he'd walked into a second-hand clothing store and purchased a pair of indigo jeans and a navy-blue roll-neck jumper; how fortunate for him the shop was open until late. "That'll be eight pounds, sir."

Danny smiled, handing over a ten-pound note. "Keep the change, mate."

The clothes looked clean and the right size, so he nipped into the changing room and put them on. He asked the sales assistant, who wore a badge displaying the name Ahmed, for a large carrier bag in which to put the black jacket and trousers.

After coffee and a burger, Danny strolled into the cinema, on a whim and watched *The Usual Suspects*. He'd enjoyed the film but found it difficult to concentrate.

The farcical and humiliating time spent in the Excelsior Club had left Danny with feelings of worthlessness. He had to admit (if only to himself) he was lonely and depressed...

Would he ever meet the girl of his dreams? That only happened on the big screen, didn't it? Not in the real world.

Chapter 2

Roxanne Elliott-Boyd

It was one of those cloudless spring mornings when you felt obliged to shield your eyes as you gazed out to sea searching the horizon for small boats…

A football rolled towards Danny, landing at his feet. He laughed and threw it back to the curly-haired child; the little boy's mother waved and smiled sweetly.

Danny leant back, needing to feel the warmth of the sun upon his face. The whisper of a salty breeze stirred his thick brown hair. He stretched, then stood up. Why not treat himself to a Cornetto? He couldn't remember the last time he'd paid for an ice-cream; he was used to helping himself from the shop's large freezer cabinet.

His father had been known to say, 'Even when times are hard, my customers call in for ice-cream, chocolate, cigarettes, crisps, newspapers and alcohol, oh – and sliced bread.' Danny would nod and laugh. 'Yes, you're absolutely right, they do, but not necessarily in that order!'

Danny strolled back towards the green bench seat, unwrapping the strawberry Cornetto on his way, pausing only to throw the wrapper in a conveniently placed litter bin. Someone was calling his name: he knew, even before turning his head, it was Rupert Gilby.

"Hi Dan, how are you doing, mate? I missed you at the party, our bloody taxi broke down, I was an hour and a half late – can you believe it? Late for my own twenty-first birthday party! I missed all the fun – so I'm told. Some weirdo popped in, dressed like Charlie Chaplin, you know, baggy trousers, socks on display, jacket far too big: must have been on drugs or got lost en route to a fancy-dress party! My mate, Ginger Etherington, sent him on his way with a barrage of sausage rolls; it must have been hilarious. All this guy lacked was a bowler hat, a cane and a moustache! They were all drunk so no-one bothered to take a photograph. Idiots. We'll never get another chance."

He smiled, his eyes lighting up in a way that made women go weak at the knees. Danny sighed, thinking, Rupert Gilby, you've never had a *real* problem in your life, have you?

Danny nodded, trying to look enigmatic. "Oh, really? How odd. Must have happened after I left. I couldn't stay long, my driving test was the following day, I had to keep a cool head.

"Oh, by the way, I'm sorry about your birthday present, I left it on the train – I nodded off and forgot all about it! I'll get you something else."

A week after Rupert's party, Danny *had* taken a driving test and passed at the first attempt so any awkward questions could have been answered quite convincingly.

"Pity you didn't get to meet Roxy, my gorgeous girlfriend – *I really think she's the one!* She'll be here, shortly. I'm thinking of proposing, what do you think, mate, too young?"

Danny grimaced – if he calls me *mate* once more, I shall say something. What's all this dumbing down crap? He didn't used to speak that way…

"Hi, darling, sorry I'm late, hope you haven't been waiting long. I couldn't find my car keys then I had trouble finding a parking space."

Danny turned; a shiver ran down his spine. For a split second, he felt nothing but hatred for his erstwhile best friend. Roxanne Elliott-Boyd was best described by two words: *sheer perfection.* Her long blonde hair had a natural wave and her big green eyes lit up when she smiled. A peachy-coloured lipstick and dark-brown mascara were all she needed to enhance her beautiful features.

A mini-skirt – faded denim, revealed a pair of long, shapely legs. Roxy looked down and smiled affectionately at her companion. Winston, a little pug, sat quietly by her side. She bent down and stroked behind his ears. "Who's a good boy, then?"

Rupert tried not to look too pleased with himself, but failed. He smiled, then introduced them. He couldn't resist saying (in a manner designed to provoke) *"Aww, look, our Danny's having an ice-cream with strawberry sauce – oh, bless him!"*

At that moment, Danny wanted nothing more than to wring Rupert's neck! Was he trying to belittle him? Had their relationship deteriorated to such an extent that Rupert thought of him now as a competitor, rather than a trusted friend? Perhaps Rupert was panicking, what if this vision of loveliness should find his old school friend more attractive or more likeable than him?

Roxy frowned. "Oh, just ignore him, sweetie, sometimes he can be a real bastard!"

She grabbed hold of Danny's Cornetto, snapped off the base then proceeded to fill it with ice-cream and strawberry sauce – thus making herself a tiny treat. "Thank you, darling." She winked at him, kissed him on the cheek, then returned his Cornetto.

Danny smiled: *I think I won that round.*

Rupert worked in the city, for Fanshawe and Peabody, merchant bankers. David Fanshawe was a good friend of Hugo Gilby and yet another poor soul who'd endured a few canings at St Wilfrid's Academy…

With plenty of new, obnoxious friends, luxury holidays, a bright red Porsche and more money than sense, it wasn't long before Rupert left his old life behind. Danny no longer recognised the shy, artistic friend he'd known and admired since their first day at school.

Danny still lived at home, with his parents, in a small semi-detached house. The rear garden was long and thin with ample room for a good size vegetable plot. Fred Dawson's fresh fruit and vegetables were legendary. The moment word got out that his new potatoes had been dug-up, runner beans had been picked or fresh strawberries and raspberries were on offer, a queue formed outside the shop…

Fred had been injured in a car accident. Working in a bespoke furniture business (with much heavy lifting) was no longer viable for this talented carpenter and joiner. For financial reasons they'd moved to a smaller house which enabled them to purchase a busy corner shop in a street with which they were familiar. It had been a sensible move: no more than five minutes' walk from Eastbourne's busy sea-front.

"Do you know something, son? I could have sold those raspberries and strawberries ten times over. If I could find a good size bit of land, I could turn it into something special. I'd start with a large building and fill it with all things garden related, you know, garden tools, mowers, bags of compost, ornaments, patio sets, indoor plants and in the summer, brightly coloured annuals like pansies and petunias. I'd continue to grow my fruit and veg, if I wasn't too busy. Just think about it – I'd be selling to far more customers. Fresh, locally grown stuff, that's what people want, I'd be on to a winner."

Fred Dawson had a faraway look as he spoke fondly of the image forming inside his head. "Up one end, I'd have a little café. Your mum loves making cakes, doesn't she? Well, she could sell slices of cake with tea or coffee and make herself a few quid."

"Yeah, great idea, dad, although I expect a few other blokes have had similar thoughts.

Still, there's nothing like that around here, or as far as I know, in the whole of East Sussex."

Danny smiled, his dad's cheeks were flushed, he'd never seen him so full of enthusiasm.

His father continued. "As you know, I enjoy listening to the radio when I'm in the shop, well, I heard something very interesting last week, on radio four's Gardeners' Question Time. One of the experts said, *'By the year two thousand, these garden centres – as people are calling them – will be springing up everywhere.'*

"That's why I need to get in quick, before someone else does. I rang your auntie Suzy yesterday. She's always saying she needs a bigger shop – well, she can have a piece of the action too. Your mum can be in one corner and your auntie in the other, they can wave to each other! According to your mum, Suzy sells good quality clothing: that'll bring in her regulars, won't it? She's so excited – loves the idea.

"Picture the scene: a lady pops in for a packet of spring bulbs then sits down and has a slice of your mum's lemon drizzle cake. Up she gets, happy as lark, walks past *'Suzy's Fabulous Fashions'* and ends up buying a couple of dresses and a beautiful leather handbag. Impulse buying, that's what they call it. *Everyone's a winner!* I'll need a small mortgage, of course, but if I get a good price for the shop, it'll be all systems go. All I have to do now is find a suitable piece of land, so come on son, keep your eyes peeled."

Fred gave a thumbs up, "All things will be considered."

As there was no need for Danny and his father to be in the shop at the same time, free deliveries to their much-appreciated customers had been on offer for several years. It was the elderly ladies who were unable drive, who really appreciated the service.

One lady, Mrs Lovage (newly widowed) came over from Bexhill-on-Sea every Friday, simply because she enjoyed the bus ride. Fred used to tease her, saying he was tempted to throw her in the back of his van, along with the vegetables and other groceries, thereby saving her the return bus fare! If things were quiet in the shop, she'd sit in the stockroom for a chat and a mug of tea. Fred said she was his favourite customer…

One day, after dropping off Mrs Lovage's groceries, Danny's eyes were drawn to a large red and white 'For Sale' board. It'd been erected behind the high, chain-link fencing that surrounded the old market garden, on the A259, four miles from Bexhill's town centre. He'd driven past it on numerous occasions but it hadn't registered as a possible site for his father's much desired garden centre. He pulled up sharply, jotting down the agent's name and telephone number. Two huge greenhouses were in a state of disrepair, they would need to be demolished and taken away. A great deal of glass had been strewn around, no doubt kids had climbed over the fence and used the greenhouses for target practice. He smiled: the glass brought back a few vivid memories.

Eleven-year-old Danny owned a catapult. During the school holidays, along with Rupert, he'd broken a few windows in derelict buildings. One day, the school bully, Wayne Pickering, had called Danny a softie. Danny had replied, "We'll soon see about that, fatso!"

The following night, just after midnight, Danny sneaked out of the house and despite being terrified, ran all the way to the school playground. With catapult in hand and a few chunky stones in his pocket, he smashed a large sash window in the science block and thoroughly enjoyed doing so! Mr Bolton, the bearded science teacher (who resembled a goat) had given Danny five hundred lines to complete by the following day: *'I must not chew gum in the classroom.'*

Danny smiled; boys will be boys...

Fred and Danny stood perfectly still, eyeing up the plot of land. At the far end, a dozen or so bags of compost could be seen along with a huge pile of topsoil, covered now with stinging nettles and dandelions. The compost must have been there for years but it was wrapped tightly in plastic so it would still be as good as new. A rusty wheelbarrow lay on its side, surrounded by an untidy pile of bricks that had once been part of the lower half of the smaller greenhouse. Dark green ivy clung to everything, searching for the light, tendrils wrapping and strangling their way around a hawthorn tree, a rowan tree and the surrounding chain-link fencing.

Fred shook his head, "Blimey, clearing this lot will be a mammoth task, I've no idea how much it will cost."

Danny agreed: before setting their hearts on it, they'd have to write down a few figures and make sure it was a viable proposition. Outlying planning permission had been granted: somewhat vague, but encouraging. They decided to put in an offer, slightly under the asking price but certainly nothing to be sneezed at.

"Come on dad, we've seen enough, let's go home. We'll ask mum to come with us to the Queens Head; if we walk round, we can all have a glass of wine. However, I won't use the word celebrate – far too soon – I don't want to jinx anything! Let's have scampi and chips, my treat. Mum can have a day off from cooking."

"Good idea, son. Your mum's a wonderful woman, she never complains and always goes along with my crazy ideas. I love her to bits…"

Fred Dawson wasn't alarmed when his mortgage application was returned. He was informed politely that, as he was over fifty, he would need to have a favourable medical carried out by his G.P. Apart from a large scar on his upper arm (due to the injury sustained in the car accident) and backache if he spent too long in the garden, he was in pretty good health.

Just like any other nervous patient, Fred's blood pressure was raised when sitting in the doctor's surgery, although it was thought to be no more than a case of 'white coat syndrome.' On this occasion, Doctor Bharat Patel informed Fred that although his blood pressure was still rather high, something else was giving greater cause for concern. Fred's cholesterol reading was off the scale. Doctor Patel nodded his head; yes, they must do something about it – today.

He suggested a new drug which was giving good results; he'd read about it in one of his medical journals. He smiled at Fred.

"After a few months on this medication, your results will be much improved and may have returned to near normal. If you don't mind me saying, if you lost twenty-eight pounds in weight, it would be most advantageous.

"Might I suggest you wait, patiently, then re-apply for that mortgage?"

Fred shook his head. *That's it, Danny, my dreams have been shattered.* I've just spoken to the mortgage broker, he said no-one will grant me a loan until my cholesterol has returned to normal. If that's gonna take several months, well, by then, someone else will have got his grubby hands on *our* piece of land. It was perfect: the right size, good location, room for a car park, and what's more – within our price range. Do you know what, son? There's not a blessed thing we can do about it."

Fred looked away; he didn't want his son to see the tears in his eyes…

Danny put a reassuring arm around his father's shoulders. "No way! We're not giving up that easily. It's your dream; we *will* make it come true.

"Hang on a minute, I do believe I've had a brainwave! I'll contact Rupert Gilby, he'll help. He's a merchant banker, that's what he does – hands out business loans. Okay, it's a tiny loan, compared to some of the stuff he handles but that's a good thing, isn't it? Cheer up, dad, how could he say no? He's known our family since he was a little kid."

David Fanshawe sniggered. "Oh, deary me. Are you serious, Rupert? Do you really think it's wise to get involved with a *minnow* like this? Some ghastly chap living in Eastbourne, having a mid-life crisis? The owner of some grubby, third-rate corner shop?

"What did you call it? A Garden *Centre?* Never heard of such a thing, sounds bloody ridiculous. One and a half acres, for what? A load of pansies, marigolds and dahlias? A few over-priced shrubs, roses, plastic watering-cans and a mower? Huh, no way. Absolutely not.

Bound to fail. In future, please don't trouble me with applications for anything less than one million pounds. You should be spending your time sorting out the Paris deal, that's where the money lies."

Rupert laughed, nervously. "Yes, of course, sir, Paris will be our crowning glory. I was feeling altruistic, that's all. To be fair, the Dawson family do run a marvellous little shop, competitive prices and extremely popular with the locals. Mr Dawson is a decent chap, salt of the earth and a good businessman. Honest as the day is long…"

Fanshaw glared at Rupert. It was obvious, his boss didn't give a damn about the Dawsons.

"Oh, yes, sorry, the Paris deal is top of my list. I shall be speaking to Gaston Dupont later today: he's their head of finance. I've studied the plans, thoroughly, even brushed up on my French! This development, just off the Champs-Elysees, sounds mind-blowing. There will be three stores: Faberge's Heritage Collection, a Jean Paul Gaultier boutique and a small, discreet, perfumery with a one-to-one highly qualified advisor. They no longer call them sales assistants! A loan of fifty-five million pounds – not Euros – has been discussed. I'm confident our interest rate will be marginally lower than the rate offered by our nearest competitors.

"Now, getting back to that other silly business, I knew Frederick Dawson's son at primary school; we were never friends, he was merely an acquaintance. I can't even recall the son's name. Damn cheek, contacting me out of the blue!"

Rupert looked over his shoulder to make sure no-one was within ear-shot: even so, he whispered the following words. "Naturally, if Fred Dawson had been one of us, a Freemason, one could safely say there might have been a more favourable outcome."

His boss looked across at him, nodded briefly, but said not a word...

Ten days later, after seeing the name of Fanshawe and Peabody printed at the top of a long white envelope, Danny, unable to wait for his parents' return, decided to rip it open. He smiled, good old Rupert. It was such a small amount of money – how could he possibly refuse? Danny had already designed the centre's logo and tagline: *A dark green cedar tree followed by:*

Dawson's Garden Centre

No-one beats our prices!

As his son was opening the envelope, Fred, accompanied by his wife, was making a special visit to Kenny's Cash and Carry; he needed to have a quiet word with the owner, Kenny Baker. During his previous visit he'd mentioned to this affable character that he was thinking of selling his corner shop. To his surprise, Kenny asked for first refusal. "Nice area, Fred – very little shop-lifting, I'm sure. I'll pay top price: I'll match any offer you get. Can't say fairer than that."

Fred sat outside the Co-op, thinking about their future. Jenny had popped inside for a large pizza marguerita, a box of chocolates and a bottle of Merlot. She'd shaken her head, no, it wasn't worth unlocking the shop for three items – she'd have to faff-about cancelling the burglar alarm and then reset it.

No-one would accuse them of being over-confident, even so, all three were feeling very excited. This time next year, Dawson's Garden Centre could be up and running: sometimes, dreams do come true…

Danny's face was pink with rage; he'd consumed three cans of strong lager which hadn't helped. He handed the letter to his father then stormed upstairs. Moments later, Queen's, *'We are the Champions'* could be heard, at full volume, with Danny joining in. His father frowned and looked across at his wife, "Oh, dear, I suppose that's supposed to be ironic."

Jenny burst into tears; this wasn't the outcome they'd been expecting. Rupert's letter was brief and to the point.

'Fanshaw and Peabody don't hand out loans to all and sundry. Merchant bankers deal with large corporations and established companies – not individuals. Might I suggest you contact the Nationwide Building Society?'

Chapter 3

Greed!

David Fanshawe sat in the waiting room, drumming his fingers impatiently on the edge of a grey plastic chair. He glanced at his watch and scowled, two-fifty, his appointment was two-thirty. Why do people (even one's private dentist) think it's perfectly acceptable to keep one waiting? He sighed, thank goodness it's only a check-up. He flicked through a copy of *Homes and Gardens* then whispered, "Can you believe it? February 1998."

The magazine was fifteen months old. A fascinating article, complete with numerous photographs, caught his eye, it had been written by popular garden expert and tv presenter, Yorkshire's finest – Alan Broadstone.

'Garden centres and why we love them!'

Alan had been invited to open a Garden Centre, a family concern, *Greenways,* five miles outside the market town of Buckingham. Smiling at his loyal fans, he'd posed, holding a huge pair of novelty scissors, made from cardboard. Once the cameras moved away, the pink ribbon was cut, with sharp scissors, by the owner…

Alan's article was full of enthusiasm.

'There's a fine display of roses: floribunda, climbing, hybrid Tea, Gallica and Bourbon. One corner has been filled with ornamental trees and small shrubs – you'll be spoilt for choice. The greenhouses are kept at a constant temperature so the young plants will be ready for the public to buy in a few months' time. Beautifully glazed pots, birdbaths and other ornamentation (for the dark corners of your garden) will have you coming back for more. I couldn't resist buying three evergreen ferns, a new variety, which I shall group together near the pond in my garden. There's a selection of wooden rose arches, or if you prefer, hand-made designs in wrought iron.

Numerous sheds too, in various sizes, and for the lady in your life, how about a delightful gazebo with small trellis attached? Perfect for a scented rose or clematis.

Where else would you find all this under one roof?

'The bright and airy restaurant was welcoming. The cheese toastie, accompanied by a light salad, was well presented. Coffee and a slice of dark chocolate cheesecake completed a delicious meal. Even if you're not a dedicated gardener, you'll love the food! A local butcher has a stall inside, alongside a ladies' dress shop. If that's not enough for you, a delicatessen has been cleverly placed, right next to the exit. Definitely a five-star experience.

'There are five newly built garden centres in England, one in Wales, one on the outskirts of Pitlochry and two in the Scottish Borders. If anyone is considering putting their money behind such an enterprise, don't think twice; you won't regret it. These wonderful centres are the future.'

David Fanshawe had been fascinated by the article, so much so, he'd ripped out the relevant pages, folded them twice then popped them inside his jacket pocket.

The following morning, Fanshawe walked straight into Rupert's office. It was just after nine-fifteen, his young protégé had yet to become embroiled in anything too challenging.

"I need to discuss something with you and when I say it's urgent, believe me, it is! Would drinks in the wine bar suit you? One o'clock?"

Rupert, as junior partner, felt obliged to defer to his boss. Nevertheless, his grovelling attitude was at times, way over the top…

He nodded, "Oh, yes, sir, that would be perfect. I must say, I'm intrigued."

Fanshawe didn't reply, instead, he hurried back to his larger, more showy office. In order to impress his wealthy clients, he'd treated himself to three original water-colour paintings: autumnal views of the Lake District. The previous week, an enormous leather sofa (pale cream) had been delivered, along with a 'top of the range' Italian coffee machine. For Fanshawe and those of his ilk, image is everything…

They arrived at the wine bar within minutes of each other. Fanshawe narrowed his eyes. "Let's grab a table, shall we? What I have to say is for your ears only. My God, if we can pull this off, we'll be loaded." After glancing round the wine bar, David handed over the article he'd torn from *Homes and Gardens,* but not as one would expect. It was passed under the table, in a rather comedic and clandestine movement.

He put a finger to his lips: "Shush, just read it – I'll get the drinks in. Glass of Merlot, is it?"

Rupert nodded. "Yes, please, sir and a bag of honey-roast cashews, *if you'd be so kind."*

David finished his double scotch and ordered another. "That middle-aged chap who lives in Eastbourne, the one with the corner shop, Frederick Dawson, isn't it? He knows his stuff. He's not as daft as we thought. I wonder, has he given up on his Garden Centre project? As his cholesterol is sky high, surely, no building society will touch him. Very bad risk…"

Rupert's cheeks were flushed. He knew exactly what his boss was thinking. They'd been longing for a scheme like this, a wholesome, guaranteed British investment, and a chance to get rich quick.

Fanshawe continued, "We'll set up a small company, registered abroad, something we can get rid of easily if things go wrong – which of course, they won't! Yes, the Cayman Islands.

"By the way, we mustn't let Eric Peacock know of our 'investment.' As you well know, he's seventy-one, had a pacemaker fitted and wouldn't approve of our tactics. I don't think he'll be coming back to work; in fact, he should have retired years ago. We may have been business partners for nigh on twenty years but as you know, he's a stickler for doing things by the book. It is for this reason only that I must keep my name out of it: how would you feel about 'Gilby Associates?'

"Oh, sounds splendid, sir, although, to be honest, I would prefer to add another couple of names. How about – um, shall we say, Gilby, Smythe and Boothroyd? It has a good, solid ring to it, sounds positively Victorian. Now then, how about this for a tagline?

Gilby, Smythe and Boothroyd

Established 1875

"A company that inspires confidence…"

Fanshawe sniggered, childishly. "Love it. Well done, my boy, you are on form today!" He patted Rupert on the back. As merchant bankers, granting themselves a loan of £400,000, was an easy task. A twenty-year loan with a fixed interest rate of just 0.25% was the icing on the cake.

Their repayments would always be 'affordable.'

The Dawsons, with a decent amount of money coming from the sale of their corner shop, had requested a mere £100,000. If granted, the loan would have been used for clearing the site, buying in stock and paying for the construction of a huge pre-fabricated metal building...

Since receiving such a patronizing and demoralizing letter from Rupert's company, it had been necessary for Fred and Danny to look straight ahead when passing the site of the old market garden. Gazing across, wistfully, was a painful reminder...

Ditches had been dug-out to improve drainage, so the surrounding area was becoming caked with mud. Temporary traffic lights were in operation, right outside the site. On this occasion, they were set to red, making it impossible for the pair to avoid looking to their left. A huge black and white sign seemed to scream at them from within the wire fence.

LAND ACQUIRED FOR CLIENTS:

Gilby, Smythe and Boothroyd

A company that inspires confidence

Fred and Danny looked at one another. "What the hell's going on?" shouted Fred, "Who are Gilby, Smythe and Boothroyd? It can't be *Rupert* Gilby, surely?"

Danny's hands felt sweaty. As luck would have it, his father was driving the van so he was able to calm himself by breathing deeply. He put his hands over his eyes, to shield them from the sun's sudden glare as it began to stream through the van's windscreen. He was getting a tension headache. As luck would have it – he found an old pair of polaroid sunglasses (belonging to his mother) in the glove compartment…

The pair walked silently through the back door; Jenny knew immediately, something was wrong. After adding crushed ice and homemade lemonade to three tall glasses, she sat down with her loved-ones, hoping to discover why they were looking angry and confused…

Danny's father had written to Rupert (his last vestiges of pride relinquished) begging for help. Was this how Rupert treated his friends? They'd asked for such a small loan, just £100,000; their much-loved shop was worth three times as much.

Why would Gilby, Smythe and Boothroyd buy a derelict piece of land on the outskirts of Bexhill-on Sea? And more to the point – who were they?

For Rupert, in his mid-twenties, buying a suitable home in London would be out of the question; he still lived in Eastbourne, with his parents, travelling to work each day by train.

It was perfectly legal for Rupert to set up a company in any name he fancied, but for Danny and Fred, something didn't feel right. The land was big enough for three or maybe four luxury homes but once the properties were sold, there would be no further investment potential.

Perhaps Rupert was designing an eco-friendly property for himself and the delectable Miss Roxanne Elliott-Boyd. He'd have one and a half acres to play with; anything was possible.

Many couples retire to the south coast and with Bexhill being such a popular seaside town, building half a dozen small bungalows, with low maintenance gardens could well be on the agenda.

Danny caught his breath – unless. He felt the blood drain from his face. Had Rupert's newly formed company decided to steal his father's long-held dream and invest in a *Garden Centre?* Was this the reason they'd refused to grant him a loan? Fred had done all the necessary leg-work for them – albeit unwittingly…

The only downside to the site was the vast quantity of asbestos sheeting and roofing tiles; a job for the professionals and they didn't come cheap. A challenge for the Health and Safety Executive too, no doubt they'd soon be sniffing round. Still, for those with limitless funds – not a problem.

If Fred Dawson had spotted articles in both the *Financial Times* and in Jenny's *Homes and Gardens* (suggesting such an investment would be a sure-fire winner) might Rupert, or his boss, David Fanshawe, have spotted them too?

Was Rupert capable of doing something so heartless and underhand to Fred Dawson, a man he'd known and respected, since he was a boy? Sadly, the answer was yes; money changes people, makes them greedy.

It was no less that a betrayal of their once unbreakable friendship.

Danny Googled *Gilby, Smythe and Boothroyd.* He drew a blank – no mention of them anywhere. Perhaps it was early days and the company had yet to achieve anything worthy of merit – this might be their first project. On the other hand, it might be a tax dodge. A merchant banker would have many tricks up his sleeve.

As Fred liked to say, 'Only working-class people pay income tax.'

Chapter 4

A very bad decision

Rupert shook his head and sighed; look at the place, what a mess. Getting rid of this lot will cost us a small fortune. He felt edgy, light-headed, he'd been too long without caffeine. He lit a cigarette and inhaled deeply. He'd prefer to be in his office, enjoying a mug of fresh coffee, chatting to colleagues or gazing down upon the view from his fifth-floor window: Westminster Bridge and the grey-green Thames…

He smiled. It's the little things you miss, like Lotus Biscoff and digestive biscuits. "Why didn't I bring a packet of biscuits with me?"

It's all very well David Fanshawe saying, *'I'll leave all the details to you, dear boy.'* What do I know about land clearance? Does a man with a van pick up everything and take it away? I'm sure that huge pile of stuff down the right-hand side is asbestos. Bad news. Isn't it classed as hazardous waste? Do I get more than one quote?

"You should get a couple of quotes for everything," he whispered, "so I've been told."

It would have been better, on that fateful day, June 30th, 1999, if Rupert had been anywhere other than on site. Strolling round aimlessly, in a state of confusion, made him look weak, vulnerable, easy prey…

A large white van screeched to a halt – two scruffy individuals jumped out and walked towards him. Both men had grins on their faces. Despite a few scratches and a light coating of mud, Rupert was able to read the sign painted on the side of their van: *P & J House Clearance. No job too small.* Underneath, a mobile phone number had been added in bright red paint, but it looked amateurish, as though added by an infantile hand…

The taller of the two was good looking and possessed the charm of the Irish. He smiled warmly. "Good mornin' to you, sir, and a fine one it is. Now then, something tells me you'll be after ridding yourself of this lot, am I right?"

Rupert felt relieved, he'd been under the impression they intended to do him harm.

He chuckled, trying to sound confident.

"Yeah, you're not kidding, mate, what a nightmare. We've got plans for this site but until this lot goes, I can't think straight."

Joseph O'Reilly nodded. "I guessed as much. I dunno, you amateurs, you're supposed to ask the professionals. That's where we come in – land clearance is our speciality. Don't mind the van, sir, that's our old one, used for house clearances. We have another van – far bigger."

His brother, Patrick, preferred to keep out of the way and say nothing, but when Joseph nodded in his direction, Patrick chimed in with his rehearsed speech. "Have you had a quote, sir?"

Rupert frowned and shook his head.

Joseph continued. "Oh, it's very bad news, sir, this lot, including the asbestos, well, that's gonna cost yer upwards of £15,000. Asbestos must be disposed of properly – they say tis made by the devil himself!

"Never fear, tis your lucky day, sir, we have all the qualifications necessary. Me and

Joseph are experts. There's a fella we know in Oxford, he takes all the asbestos we recover, double bags it then buries it in a special landfill site – all legal and above board. He's a good fella, so he is."

Even though his brain was sending out warning signals, Rupert chose to ignore them – preferring to see Patrick and Joseph O'Reilly as no more than lovable rogues...

"Will we be getting the job, sir? Shall we say, £6,000, for cash? Oh yes, tis a fair offer."

How he wished there was someone knowledgeable standing beside him, someone who knew about land clearance. He wasn't happy making decisions about things way outside his comfort zone. Unfortunately, his father, Hugo, was useless with *anything* that didn't involve making or acquiring vast sums of money.

Fred Dawson's opinion would have been most welcome, if nothing else, he'd have known if the quote was a reasonable one.

Danny seemed to have drifted away, it was as if a brick wall had been erected between them. Had he said or done something to upset him?

He studied the men standing before him: their attitude had hardened. It was easier for Rupert to say yes, than upset them. "Okay, yes, I suppose so. When can you collect all the stuff?"

"Well sir, tomorrow lunch-time will suit us fine. *Make sure you have the money ready.*"

The O'Reilly brothers stood unnecessarily close to Rupert, hands on hips, staring at him. He was under the impression they were warning him not to be difficult. They nodded, hurried towards the van then drove away at high speed...

A row of red-brick terraced houses backed onto the site, each garden long and narrow.

Alice Hoskins shouted from the bottom of the stairs. "Lucinda! I told you to bag-up your rubbish and put it in the wheelie bin, have you done it? No! Your bedroom is still like a tip. If you expect pocket-money, then damn well earn it. By the way, your dinner will be ready in twenty minutes."

The Hoskins family lived at number twenty-seven Wilberforce Terrace. From her bedroom window, thirteen-year-old Lucinda had a good view of the site, she frowned, what an eye-sore. Surely all that asbestos stuff shouldn't be left there, should it? Wasn't it dangerous? She'd have to ask her dad; he knew about these things.

Lucinda put a pile of unwanted things on her dressing table, including a couple of cheap, cotton T shirts – ruined by her stupid mother – she'd let them shrink in the wash. These items were destined for the charity shop. She'd take the stuff downstairs when *she* felt like it and not before. As usual her mum was making a fuss about nothing…

Lucinda's bedroom window was open wide: in the height of summer the room became stifling. A small plastic carrier bag, displaying the words, *Boots pharmacy,* had been left on the window sill; it rustled in the breeze. The bag had no weight to it as it contained no more than an empty packet of Maltesers, make-up remover pads (covered with mascara) and a few lengths of dental floss. A sales receipt had been left in the bottom of the carrier bag, along with a bus ticket for two-pounds and fifty-pence. Mrs Hoskins' Visa card had been debited with sixteen pounds and forty-nine pence, at eleven o'clock, the previous Thursday. The transaction took place at store number 374, located in Devonshire Road, Bexhill, East Sussex.

Suddenly, the wind increased to such a degree, a pile of dry leaves (raked up and left beside the lawn) swirled to a height of almost two metres. The Hoskins' cat, Maurice, found this event quite disturbing; he returned to the kitchen immediately, via his cat-flap. He didn't like windy days: even a warm summer breeze made him bad-tempered…

Just as Maurice was climbing through his cat-flap, the Boots carrier bag took flight; out of the bedroom window it went, swooping and diving until it landed inside the derelict site. A dead branch, snapped off by this mini tornado, fell on top of the carrier bag, pinning it to a sheet of asbestos: the bag was going nowhere!

Rupert arrived at the site just after midday. The O'Reilly brothers suggested lunch time – not particularly helpful – they might not arrive until two o'clock. David Fanshawe had insisted, 'Take the day off, no problem, the sooner we get the site cleared, the better. There's a lot of money riding on this, so don't cock it up!'

By twelve-thirty, Rupert had finished his M&S smoked ham and cheese sandwiches. He'd been looking forward to a bar of chocolate-covered marzipan, but found it extremely disappointing, much too sweet. How about less sugar and more ground-almonds?

He sat back in his mum's new, Nissan Micra, trying to get comfortable, hoping to have a nap. Only an idiot would let the O'Reilly brothers catch sight of a bright red Porsche! He smiled, luckily, the previous day, he'd parked the Porsche round the corner, in Wilberforce Terrace.

He jumped; someone was hammering on the windscreen! Two faces glared at him…

Rupert climbed out of the car and offered the men a cigarette – they both grabbed one, eagerly, delighted to see they were Marlborough gold, king size. Three youths ran over from the second van, one looked across at Rupert, but when offered a cigarette, he shook his head, instead, laughing now, he grabbed the packet. He threw it in the direction of the youngest boy who looked no more than thirteen. The curly-haired boy lit a cigarette and inhaled deeply, causing laughter from his family. Joseph slapped his nephew on the back, *"Ah, well done, Callum, we'll make a man of you, so we will!"*

The vans were filled with broken glass, a couple of hacked-down elderberry bushes, a rowan tree, two small tree trunks, greenhouse frames, a broken wheelbarrow, paving slabs, several piles of bricks and a pile of topsoil.

Rupert paced up and down then sat in the car, waiting for the men to return. He assumed they'd been to a local site, one that accepted trade waste, for a fee. In reality they'd driven to a friend's small-holding, near Hastings and deposited the waste which would be picked up at a future date.

"Well, that's it, sir," said Patrick. "That's £6,000 you owe us, unless you want the asbestos removed."

Rupert looked puzzled. "What d'you mean? Surely, that was part of the deal? £6,000 *included* the removal of the asbestos."

Joseph narrowed his eyes. "There's one thing I will not tolerate – someone trying to cheat us out of our hard-earned cash. If you want to say goodbye to that asbestos, it'll cost you another three grand. You seem to have forgotten, we're taking it all the way to Oxford, a specially licensed landfill site, it'll cost us a fortune. There's nowhere round here, they've all closed down. Oh, by the way, I remember you saying there'd be a hundred quid each, for the lads. *So, I make that £9,300, am I right?"*

Patrick stood next to his brother, brandishing a monkey wrench, his expression anything but friendly…

Rupert had been standing in the bank's lengthy queue when something in the back of his mind told him to get a cool £10,000. He opened his briefcase slowly – his hands shaking. Such a vast amount of cash. The large brown envelope was thrust towards Patrick.

"There's ten grand, you greedy bastards," he shouted, *"take the bloody lot! Happy now?"*

Patrick's eyes lit up, he smiled warmly and chuckled. "Ah, that's most kind of you, so it is… I won't insult you by counting it. We'll load up the asbestos then we'll be on our way. You'll not be seeing us again, sir, so I'll bid you good-day."

Rupert was shattered, his head was banging and he felt nauseous. He found an unopened bottle of mineral water in the glove compartment. "Thanks mum," he whispered.

He drove slowly towards Eastbourne, feeling cramped and uncomfortable inside his mother's Micra. Although the driver's seat had been pushed back as far as it would go, his legs still seemed far too long. Sainsbury's superstore loomed in front of him, he signalled, then pulled into the car park. Three items were needed – one being a small bottle of brandy. He wasn't a fan of the stuff but once home, he'd be pouring himself a double. After picking up a box of painkillers, he went to the kiosk and asked for twenty Marlborough gold, king size, then added, "No, better make that two packs. Cheers."

He winked at the pretty young cashier.

Wow, she thought, I hope he comes in again, he is gorgeous…

The lying, cheating Irishmen – or whatever Rupert chose to call them – had nicked all his cigarettes. He hated the O'Reilly brothers and 'the lads' with a passion. Why was his stomach still in knots? It seemed to be telling him, 'Don't be naïve, this isn't over, you haven't seen the last of them.'

A week later, Mrs Gilby and Mrs Dawson came face to face…

The moment she'd spotted Alicia in Dorothy Perkins, examining a new range of lacy underwear, Jenny decided to leave the store. They'd never been close friends – why pretend otherwise? As she approached the exit, a pink and white striped cotton blouse caught Jenny's eye. She was searching for a size twelve when Alicia crept up behind her, making her jump. "Oh, Jenny, how very nice to see you."

Mrs Gilby looked uncomfortable; she could detect an iciness in Mrs Dawson's expression. Jenny didn't reply, she just nodded her head, intending to move away…

"Can I buy you a coffee, dear? There's something I need to explain."

Ignoring Alicia's patronizing tone, Jenny shrugged her shoulders, "I suppose so."

They crossed the road and walked slowly towards Alfonso's, a pretentious and rather over-hyped venue. Neither lady was capable of conjuring-up a smile…

"Rupert told me he had no choice, he had to turn down your husband's request for a loan. Well, let me assure you, my son was most upset, he told us all about it, over lunch, he's such a sensitive soul. The thing is, Fanshawe and Peabody would *never* grant a small loan like that, they are merchant bankers, moving millions of pounds from place to place on a daily basis. There's a deal going on at the moment, in Paris, a small luxury development, just off the Champs Elysees. Rupert will be flying out again next week. His boss, David Fanshawe, is *very* fond of him, trusts him implicitly."

Alicia loved boasting about her son's dubious achievements...

The coffee was good, but the cake was disappointing: mass produced, dry and with barely a tang of fresh lemon juice. Jenny's version of lemon drizzle cake was topped with thick, lemony icing and so moist you couldn't resist a second slice.

She felt miserable; why couldn't she stop thinking about the exciting plans she'd made for the garden centre café? She mustn't torture herself, what was the point? It was never going to happen.

Alicia finished her coffee then continued with her one-sided conversation. "Now then, where was I? Oh yes, of course, the development on the A259. No doubt you've seen the board, Gilby, Smythe and Boothroyd, one of their smaller companies. Rupert and David felt they wanted to *give something back'* to the community, so they came up with a rather splendid idea – affordable housing.

"In a strange twist of fate, one could say it was all down to your husband – Frederick, isn't it? Yes, he brought the derelict sight to their attention.

"Rupert said there's room for five low-maintenance detached bungalows with courtyard-style gardens. Perfect for anyone newly retired. Such a lovely idea, so much nicer than one of those enormous garden centres. I'm not afraid to say it, Jennifer, although we have yet to visit one, we think they are ghastly, vulgar places. Besides, weekends on that part of the A259 would become a nightmare! Who knows, a garden centre might cause traffic jams or even accidents if too many people were trying to turn into the car park. Imagine it, all those strangers coming from who knows where. Oh, yes, my son made the right decision."

Jenny had been biding her time. She glared at Alicia.

"Oh, you think so, do you? I would have thought building a garden centre, something new and exciting for the locals to enjoy, would also be '*giving something back.*' Think about it for a moment – plenty of parking spaces, ideal for the elderly or disabled. Everything you need for the garden, a café, a good quality clothes shop and other outlets, all under one roof. It would've created dozens of jobs, full-time, part-time, students who need to work during the holidays, and mums with kids who want to earn a few quid. Bexhill is hardly short of bungalows, is it? Five more, built by your son's new company, won't make a scrap of difference."

Jenny's voice became louder. A couple of elderly ladies, on the next table, frowned, but listened nevertheless.

"Fred is heartbroken, this was his long-held dream. He'll never find another piece of land so close to home. It was perfect, and more to the point, with a very small loan from

Fanshaw and Peabody – we could have afforded it!"

Jenny stood up and walked away, not bothering to say goodbye. It wasn't until she was halfway home that she realised she hadn't paid for her coffee and cake. She smirked. It'd been Alicia's idea, she can pay, snooty cow, she's loaded…

Chapter 5

A despicable crime

It was the first day of the school holidays and just two weeks after the O'Reilly brothers cleared all the debris (including the huge pile of asbestos sheets and tiles) from the site on the A259.

For two young boys, Simon and Ian, these were the days they'd remember when they grew old and frail; a time to go outside, explore and seek adventure in the real world. It was a time to buy sweets and fizzy drinks, ride their bikes, climb trees and make camps. Their favourite pastime was following (at a safe distance) anyone who looked like a foreign spy. The previous day they'd spotted a very dodgy-looking character; the boys agreed, he certainly looked like a spy, the worst possible type – *a Russian spy!*

Who else would grow a thick ginger beard, wear horn-rimmed spectacles and a shabby beige raincoat with the collar turned up? Perhaps the beard was false. They'd followed him from Wendover Court to Aylesbury

Terrace, a distance of three quarters of a mile. Why was this man, whom they'd never seen before, putting colourful catalogues through people's letter boxes? Perhaps one of the catalogues contained a secret message sent from Moscow, concealed within the pages!

According to the boys' mother, the poor man had a tedious job selling *Betterware* household products. His name was Jeff and he lived in one of the ground-floor flats in Birchwood Court. She'd spoken to him when ordering a tin of lavender polish for the dining-room table.

"I can confirm, hand on heart, Jeff Robbins is *not* a Russian spy." She looked sad. "Perhaps, if he was, they'd be rich! Sadly, his young wife, Sharon, is in a wheelchair and he's her main carer…"

The boys shrugged, perhaps they weren't as clever as they thought they were. They'd argue, occasionally, but usually agreed on one thing, to ignore any words of wisdom or advice handed out by their parents.

It was eight o'clock; the boys had finished their Weetabix. This morning, for a change, it was topped with sliced banana and maple syrup. Jeanette Henderson asked her sons if they'd like to take Marji for her first walk of the day. Marji was a three-year old Border terrier, inquisitive but obedient enough to walk alongside the boys...

In its heyday, Mill Lane had been a very busy place. Horses and carts traipsed up and down the muddy track carrying sacks full of wholemeal, or if preferred, the more desirable white flour. The mill supplied flour to Lower Foxton and several other small villages on the outskirts of Oxford...

To everyone's dismay the mill closed down in 1967, but the structure remained, despite being in a state of disrepair. A two-metre-high fence had been erected around the building, complete with warning notice. The bright-red letters were clear for all to see:

DANGER – KEEP OUT. However, it did nothing to deter the local children. Despite parents forbidding their offspring from entering this once beautiful windmill, they managed to climb over the fence, or cut a hole in the wire and squeeze through. The windmill was at the far end of the lane, just over a mile from the main road. The ground behind it sloped away, quite steeply, leading to nothing more interesting that a deep ditch. Now, through neglect, the ditch was almost hidden by brambles, ferns and wild garlic. Sometimes, in the spring, sticklebacks could be seen beneath the surface, searching for their favourite prey, tadpoles…

The young boys were almost speechless. The ditch had been filled with rubbish – why? Who would do such a shocking thing?

Despite wearing his wellies, Ian couldn't resist running down the slope at high speed with his arms outstretched – he had to investigate.

"Si, quick, come and look at all this stuff!"

Simon raced down the slope to join his brother, then scowled. What a mess! A huge pile of bricks, broken glass, paving slabs, tree trunks and two huge twisted metal frames…

The O'Reilly brothers had been busy: two more house clearances had been carried out, their contents scattered alongside all the debris from the site on the A259. Both vans had been reversed, back doors opened wide and their contents kicked, thrown or rolled down the slope. A stained, mock-leather sofa plus two equally filthy armchairs (in lime green) a single mattress, tv, rusty fridge-freezer, a kitchen stool and a broken motor-mower, made the area look more like a council tip…

There'd been laughter from the adults and a great deal of alcohol consumed by the lads. Well, why not? At three o'clock in the morning, you could make as much noise as you pleased! No-one could hear or see them.

Patrick always carried a bottle of Irish whiskey in the van. Drink driving? Why not? He was a good driver: he knew what he was doing. The O'Reilly brothers made their own rules. One set of keys, belonging to the dark-blue transit van, was thrown in the direction of fourteen-year-old Callum. Joseph had laughed and slapped him on the back. "Go on then, me boy, let's see what your driving's like – you can be our taxi home…"

Ian Henderson wandered off, intrigued by a third pile of rubbish; he turned and shouted to his brother. "What's all this white powdery stuff? It's great, it looks like snow!"

It was sheer good fortune that the previous week the boys' father, Jimmy Henderson, had become agitated whilst watching a television documentary introduced by the ever-popular investigative journalist, Peter Shelby. *'The White Stuff!'* had been a lengthy investigation into the illegal dumping of asbestos by unscrupulous individuals. Sadly, this appalling crime was more common than one might imagine. Simon had walked into the living room just as his parents were 'letting off steam' and expressing their anger at the evidence provided. Dozens of photographs had been taken by a BBC cameraman, from a number of illegal sites, mainly in the south and east of England. All evidence had been passed to the police and the Health and Safety Executive.

"Ian, don't touch anything!" shouted his brother, *"It's lethal! Don't unclip Marji's lead, either!"*

Ian had picked up a long, thin branch, brought down by the wind, his intention being to smash-up the pile of asbestos tiles. His actions would have released a cloud of deadly, snowy-white fibres; many would have become trapped in his healthy young lungs…

Simon's words unnerved him. He threw down the branch and dashed over to join his brother.

Simon continued, "Listen to me, Ian. Dad was talking about asbestos a few days ago. Mum and dad had been watching a programme about it. It's evil stuff, gives you cancer – you must never touch it or poke at it with a stick. *Understand?* We'd better tell the police, *right now!* They must be told, mustn't they?"

Ian felt scared, vulnerable. Why couldn't they go home and ask their mum to telephone the police? He nodded, "Okay, then." He knew Simon was right, they must go to the police station immediately, otherwise something really bad might happen, something they could have prevented! Who on earth would dump dangerous stuff where children, dogs, cats and wild animals could find it?

Simon and Ian walked up the steps and through the double doors of Lower Foxton's small, rural police station. They were nervous until they noticed the friendly smile of the Desk Sergeant. "Hello, lads, what can I do for you?"

Sergeant Wilcox was shocked when he heard of the boys' discovery. "Really? Asbestos? Goodness me, that's evil stuff. Wait here, lads, I'll make a quick phone call; we'll send someone out there immediately. They'll need to close off Mill Lane. Yes, plenty of blue and white tape." He scratched his chin. "I'll phone the local radio station – they'll broadcast a warning."

Sergeant Wilcox's cheeks were flushed, he'd never come across anything like this before. "That asbestos will have to be removed by experts. When I tell the Inspector you've been in to see us, I'm sure he'll put your names forward for some sort of award. You might have saved a few lives, even your little dog's life. Well done boys."

Alfie Wilcox opened the top drawer of his desk. He was on a strict diet, so he was more than happy to hand over two bars of Galaxy milk chocolate. He sighed: *better them than me.*

"Oh, I'll need your names and addresses, telephone numbers too, for your parents…"

He grinned at the boys. "Oh dear, I'm a bit slow on the uptake today – I can see it now – you are brothers, aren't you? A good deal younger than my two lads! Now then, you'll both have to give us a written statement, which means, you'll need someone called a 'responsible adult' with you. Can mum or dad come in and sit with the pair of you?"

Chapter 6

Indisputable evidence

Since leaving university, Robert Musgrove had worked for the Health and Safety Executive. He'd been called out twice the previous week, leaving him over-tired and short-tempered. Due to the lack of successful prosecutions, the illegal tipping of waste was once again on the increase and therefore high on the agenda.

A number of England's delightful country lanes had been turned into illegal tips. If just one person left a pile of rubbish, others would follow, as if they had some God-given right to pollute and destroy these fragile habitats. It wasn't just the mountain of fridges and televisions, filthy sofas and stained mattresses – people living close-by had to put up with the appalling smell – especially during spring and summer. Huge rats had moved in; these illegal tips were becoming breeding grounds. Something drastic needed to be done…

This morning, Robert was taking the new girl with him, 'It'll be a learning experience,' said Mr Haslam, the boss, 'nothing like being out there at the coal face.' What a ridiculous thing to say. Robert thought his boss was an idiot.

A couple of young lads had walked into Lower Foxton police station and caused quite a stir. The boys had said, 'Judging by the muddy tyre tracks, *two* vans had been reversed and the contents chucked out.' Most of it had rolled or been thrown down the slope and into the deep muddy ditch. One pile of debris contained a great deal of asbestos, which was no laughing matter…

Although Emily Brown looked no more than twenty, Robert knew she must be a few years older. She'd been awarded an Honours degree in Environmental Studies and Geophysics. After the interviews had taken place, the panel agreed, Emily was head and shoulders above all the other candidates. Robert had to admit, she was a very attractive young lady: long dark hair, big brown eyes and a delightful enthusiasm for her chosen career. If only he were single and ten years younger…

His thoughts turned to 'her indoors,' Mrs Elaine Musgrove – what a nightmare. He knew she was sleeping with another man, it was blindingly obvious. He didn't know who it was, although he had his suspicions. Since she'd been employed by *Wilkins and Bramwell,* based in Wallingford, they'd grown apart. It was one those snooty agencies, the type who think they're a cut above the rest simply because they've been in business since the 1950s. They'd made more than enough money to ensure their staff had brand-new, top of the range cars. Elaine was driving a brand-new mini, black, very smart, she loved it. She'd admitted to Robert, quite shamelessly, she told everyone it was her own car, the boss had given it to her for being their top salesperson the previous year.

Robert wondered if Elaine had enough to keep her occupied, her working day had been reduced to six hours plus every other Saturday morning. Perhaps, since the arrival of Rightmove, she had too much time on her hands.

She started to wear an unusual colour lipstick, burgundy, it didn't suit her, she looked as if she'd devoured a bowl of black cherries. Occasionally, a smudge of lipstick strayed onto her teeth – definitely not a good look. Previously, she'd worn a shade of pink. Elaine was spending a fortune at the hairdressers (always worrying about her dark roots) although Robert had to admit, blonde hair made her look softer, prettier.

Before changing jobs, Elaine gave very little thought to her appearance; no wonder he'd become suspicious. He was thirty-three and so was his wife, but on occasions, he wondered if life was passing him by…

Wearing their Hi-Viz protective gear, Robert and Emily Brown examined the area surrounding the windmill, taking special note of the deep, muddy ditch. Robert shook his head, what was the matter with these people? Fly tipping of any sort made him angry, but when he saw asbestos, he felt his blood pressure rise. Kids played in Mill Lane, people walked their dogs and what about the wildlife? Emily called his name, he turned around. She'd found something of interest, she held it up for Robert to see. He hurried over to join her. It was a flattened carrier bag with Boots written across the middle in dark blue letters – a small knot had been tied at the top. Emily had spotted it poking out from beneath a pile of asbestos roofing tiles. It must have been shovelled up along with all the other rubbish.

"Oh, well done, Emily." Robert smiled warmly at his new protégé. Many clues could be discovered inside a grubby carrier bag. The bag contained an empty packet of Maltesers, make-up remover pads (covered with mascara) and a few lengths of dental floss. A sales receipt had been left in the bottom of the carrier bag, along with a dated, screwed-up bus ticket for two-pounds and fifty-pence. Somebody's Visa card had been debited with sixteen pounds and forty-nine pence. The date and time of transaction were printed clearly on the sales receipt, next to a Boots' loyalty card number. This particular branch of Boots, store number 374, was located in Devonshire Road, Bexhill-on-sea, East Sussex. Good gracious: the asbestos had travelled way over one hundred miles!

Robert raised his eyebrows and nodded. The Boots' receipt would provide the necessary details to enable the bank in question to provide him with the information he so desperately needed…

The following Friday afternoon, Mrs Hoskins and Lucinda, number twenty-seven Wilberforce Terrace, received a visit from Robert and Emily. Fancy driving all the way from Oxford to Bexhill, just to interview *them!* Mother and daughter found the whole situation intriguing. The items found inside Lucinda's small, Boots' carrier bag, were valuable evidence. Mr Musgrove said the likelihood of the asbestos coming from anywhere other than the derelict site at the back of their garden, must be a million to one.

"Wow!" said Lucinda, after examining the photographs on Emily's phone, "Yeah, that my carrier bag, alright, deffo. It was on the window sill, I wondered what happened to it. I guessed it'd blown over the fence into all that mess, so I wasn't bothered. I'd left my bedroom window open, cos it was ever so hot that evening…"

After eating a slice of Mrs Hoskins delicious carrot cake (made especially for the occasion) Robert and Emily headed back to Oxford, hoping to avoid the worst of the evening's traffic. One hundred and thirty miles; three hours and forty minutes, if they were lucky. Robert glanced across at Emily. "A long journey but worth it. Quite an odd situation. The owner, or owners of the land, will be given a massive fine, anything up to £20,000 *and* they'll have to pay the cost of removing the asbestos from Mill Lane. Who knows, it could be almost as much again. That's what happens when you cut corners. The fine will be less if they give us the name of the contractor. Probably gypsies, in which case, the owners will be too scared to pass on their names. Anyway, fancy stopping for a coffee? The carrot cake was very tasty but sugary things tend to make me thirsty."

Emily smiled flirtatiously at Robbie; there was nothing she'd like more.

The previous evening she'd said to her sister, "Robbie Musgrove, who's teaching me the ropes, well, he's ever so attractive. I'm going out with him tomorrow. Work, not pleasure, I hasten to add.

"Someone has dumped a load of rubbish in Mill Lane, Lower Foxton. Asbestos too – that's a shocking thing to do, it's carcinogenic. Do you remember going there, years ago, with mum and dad? We took our first dog, Lucky. Yes, I could remember the windmill. You should see it now – it's no more than a wreck.

"Anyway, tomorrow, we're driving down to Bexhill-on-sea, East Sussex, we need to see where all the rubbish came from and interview a couple of people.

"Oh, Trish, what am I gonna do? I don't half fancy him. Aren't I awful? I wonder if he's married? He hasn't mentioned a wife, not once."

"Oh, don't be such an idiot, Ems, you said he's much older than you, he's bound to be married. There lies trouble."

Emily sighed, "Yeah, but…"

"Yeah, but nothing!" cut in her sister, "He'd only want you for one thing."

Emily blushed, "Well, I'd be after the same thing; it's time I lost my virginity."

Trish looked wide-eyed. Despite being in her twenties, she couldn't resist giving her sister a playful poke in the ribs. "Cor, don't you let mum hear you say that, she'd go absolutely nuts."

Chapter 7

Devious plans

Rupert's mother looked tired and anxious; she was holding a large glass of Sherry. "Your father is looking for you, my dear. He's in the study."

Hugo narrowed his eyes; he couldn't resist waving a copy of the Eastbourne Gazette in front of his son. "You've certainly ruffled a few feathers, my boy, pages two and three, plus a black and white photograph – it must have been taken years ago. Bloody journalists! They're all troublemakers, why didn't they add a photograph of you standing next to the lovely Roxy?

A note of sarcasm crept into Hugo's voice. *"Oh, I nearly forgot, there's the small matter of a £20,000 fine and a clear-up fee of £10,500. The name of Gilby has been dragged through the mud. What the hell were you thinking of?"*

Rupert gazed at the delicate pattern on the new burgundy and cream carpet. Replying to his father's forthright comments would not be wise or even expected. He'd apologised, numerous times. What more did his parents want? Blood?

Hugo removed a pale-grey cheque book from the desk drawer. He sighed. "Mark my words, this is the first and only time I shall bail you out."

He filled his gold-nibbed Waterman fountain pen with turquoise ink. The pen was kept for special occasions and used when signing birthday and Christmas cards. Today, Hugo needed the comfort provided by the pen's beauty and opulence. Besides, it gave his hand-writing a certain style. After dabbing his signature with a piece of torn-off blotting paper, he passed the cheque to his wayward son.

"There's only one way out of this ghastly situation. You may not care about local gossip, but your mother certainly does. You will contact Daniel Dawson and invite him and his father over for drinks. They're not *our* sort of people, of course, but needs must...

"You can suggest we join forces, let's call it a working partnership, fifty-fifty, straight down the middle. With Frederick's knowledge of all things garden related, and our flair for business, perhaps we can drag something positive out of this ghastly mess. Make sure you have a few words with David Fanshawe, apologise, say we won't be needing him now. I'm sure he'll be over the moon. He'll not wish to be tarnished by your incompetence. If all goes according to plan, the Dawsons will be buying Fanshawe's half of the investment."

Hugo finished his glass of Merlot, lit a cigar, then chuckled. "I've just had a rather splendid idea. Once things are up and running, we'll spread a few juicy rumours, it was *Daniel's* idea, not yours, to do things on the cheap. He telephoned the O'Reilly brothers and asked for a quote – you knew nothing about it until it was too late.

"We'll say Daniel had laughed – treating it as a joke – when telling you Patrick and Joseph were no less than conmen. He could tell they were *very* dodgy, he'd no idea where they were taking the rubbish and to be honest, for £10,000 – he couldn't care less!

"Daniel failed to tell you they'd removed a considerable amount of highly carcinogenic asbestos from the site, oh yes. As no-one of any consequence is aware Fanshawe and Peabody refused to give the Dawsons a loan, people will assume a partnership between our families was planned months ago. Oh, by the way, as *Gilby, Smythe and Boothroyd* is no more than a tax dodge, for goodness-sake, take down that ridiculous sign!"

Alicia felt anxious and depressed; their precious holiday fund had been raided in order to pay the huge fine and clear-up fee. More to the point, she'd found it necessary to resign from the W.I., Eastbourne branch. The thought of facing all fifty-seven members after such a fiasco made her feel physically sick. *Was it possible to die from embarrassment?*

She closed her eyes, trying to make sense of what had taken place. I can hardly believe it, my son, getting involved with gypsies! Alicia was horrified, Lower Foxton was on the margins of the Cotswolds, an area favoured by the royals and no more than forty miles from Highgrove. She swallowed another couple of strong painkillers.

"My precious son does have one flaw," she whispered, "he can be naïve at times, he lets people take advantage of him. Thank goodness he didn't accompany the O'Reilly brothers to Lower Foxton, that would have made him an accomplice."

Alicia poured herself another glass of sherry and settled down with the Daily Telegraph. Perhaps attempting such a challenging crossword would help her relax. She sighed, what was the point? She couldn't concentrate but it wasn't her fault; no, of course it wasn't. For some unknown reason, the nasty crossword compiler had decided to make the clues extra difficult to solve.

The alcohol was making Alicia behave irrationally. She sprang out of her armchair: the folded newspaper was hurled across the room followed swiftly by the glass, which, after missing a valuable Tiffany lamp, landed on a thick cream-coloured Persian rug. A huge, ugly stain appeared, deep reddish-brown, her husband would be furious.

She'd have to tell a lie, yes, she'd tripped over the edge of the rug. Luckily, she'd managed to grab hold of an armchair, so, apart from the sherry stain – no harm done. Why not blame Mrs Gladwin, the cleaner? Brilliant! The woman must have disturbed the rug when vacuuming the carpet and left it rucked up. *Careless; dangerous too.*

Alicia threw back her head and laughed. She knew exactly what to say to her husband…

'Don't worry, darling, I'll have a word with Mrs Gladwin. The rug will need dry-cleaning. I'm aware she's arthritic and needs the money, but even so, I shall take the cost out of her wages. If it wasn't for the shortage of cleaning women, I'd damn well sack her.'

Alicia had spent months and quite a lot of money cultivating a budding friendship between herself and Lady Cynthia Winthrop. The previous week, she'd booked a spa day at Friston Hall and Golf Club: a surprise sixtieth birthday present for Lady Cynthia, Eastbourne's most prominent socialite.

Perhaps, if she telephoned Friston Hall immediately, she could cancel the booking and they'd return her deposit – after all, it wasn't until the following month. Lady Cynthia would be none the wiser…

The thought of getting together with a group of friends and acquaintances was too much to contemplate. What if someone should make a spiteful comment regarding Rupert's recent 'exploits?' What if she over-heard the dreaded word, asbestos? She couldn't run away from Friston Hall wearing a snowy white bath robe!

Failing to acknowledge her own personality traits, Alicia found Cynthia arrogant and lacking in empathy. Nevertheless, being friends with a lady from such an esteemed family helped raise her own profile. One day they might receive a much-desired invitation, lunch at Winthrop Manor, a stunning 16th century Tudor masterpiece, displaying some of the finest herringbone brickwork in England.

Family records provided written evidence (if proof were needed) that Queen Elizabeth I slept under the roof of Winthrop Manor, for two nights, during the long, cold winter of 1568. Over one thousand pounds was spent on food, lavish entertainment and the challenge of finding extra accommodation for her majesty plus her large retinue of servants. Some of the lower ranked servants slept in the stables: they were permitted one blanket each. As it was so cold, they snuggled up to the horses who gave out some warmth…

Queen Elizabeth had been impressed by the showy and meat-inspired banquet.

An enormous turducken – a boned chicken, stuffed into a boned duck which is then stuffed into a boned turkey – was the centrepiece. The final course of this eight-course meal was a syllabub. Thick double cream with added sherry, honey and the grated rind and juice from oranges and lemons. After such a generous banquet, Her Majesty felt obliged to bestow a knighthood upon Peregrine Winthrop.

If Cynthia had been given a pound every time she'd re-told this elaborate tale, she'd have a pile of coins stretching to the ceiling...

Lord Basil Winthrop was a member of the House of Lords but sat in the chamber only when an important vote was taking place. However, he was eager to claim his expenses. He thought three-hundred and twenty-three pounds per day was a miserly offering. How was he expected to entertaining businessmen or colleagues without dipping into his own money? On occasions, he'd sign in at the Lords, stay for an hour, listen to a few boring speeches (followed by drinks with fellow peers of the realm) then move on to the Excelsior club, with its superior wine cellar.

Chapter 8

An unlikely partnership

Jenny Dawson had never been a big fan of alcohol; anything more than one glass of wine would trigger a bad headache. It was for this reason she'd offered to drive Fred and Danny to the Gilby's home. Although she hadn't been invited, this so-called meeting was something she dare not miss, even as a casual observer. They arrived at ten-past-seven.

"Perfect timing," announced Fred, looking confident, "no-one wants their guests to turn up early."

The houses in Balmoral Drive were built between the wars, impressive dwellings with five bedrooms and three bathrooms: even now, they possessed an air of faded grandeur. In 1932, for the upper classes, a double garage and large conservatory would seem perfectly normal. As servants were still paid a pittance, they were yet to be considered a luxury...

"Do come through to the garden," said Hugo, ushering them towards the side gate.

The rear garden of 'The Oaks' had a large, circular lawn with a weed-free flower-bed in the centre. The evening was warm and humid. A wren sang from within the dense beech hedging: a sweet, melodious sound. A display of cottage-garden plants turned their heads eagerly towards the evening sun. Fred thought the chocolate-coloured sunflowers were stunning; maybe next year, he'd be selling some from his very own garden centre. The hollyhocks were impressive too – every shade imaginable from pale pink through to deepest burgundy.

The perimeter of the garden had been covered with grey slate – its colour enhanced by the addition of several ornamental trees. In one corner an arbutus (known as the *strawberry tree)* was doing well, its fruits ranging from green to amber, although some had ripened to a deep red. Fred could name every tree and shrub in the garden although Danny and his mum were less knowledgeable.

Alicia pointed towards a recent purchase: a group of five acers – their leaves in shades of lime green, deep tangerine and burgundy.

Jenny had an acer, in a pot by the front door. She smiled to herself: it was small and rather pathetic although she could remember paying twenty-five pounds for it. No doubt the Gilby's acers had a very hefty price-tag.

Where spending money was concerned, the Gilbys didn't hold back. *'One must always create a good impression,'* was Alicia's favourite saying...

Hugo suggested moving to the pergola; he'd noticed a few midges. Alicia asked Jenny to give her a hand with the drinks' trolley. A home-made pecan pie was on offer, or if preferred, a choice of savoury snacks.

Fred longed to say, 'Never mind all this fancy stuff, delicious though it is, can we get down to business, please?'

After two slices of pie, topped with clotted cream, the atmosphere became less frosty; a few smiles and even a little warmth could be detected.

Danny felt ill at ease in Rupert's company, yet they'd once been as close as brothers. They moved away from the pergola and walked self-consciously around the garden. Danny stopped by the pond to admire a fine display of Koi Carp. Rupert found a football, behind the shed, in a small area of long grass.

Two young men, playing football; it wasn't long before one of them kicked the ball over the fence and into a neighbour's garden, reminding them of their childhood, which seemed to reignite their friendship. They sat on the wooden bench seat, reliving some of their shared memories…

"Remember when you smashed that sash window in the science block, with your catapult? Mr Bolton went mad. Everyone knew it was you. It was so cool, you lucky devil – no-one grassed you up!"

Danny chuckled. "How could I forget? That was my finest hour. I needed to impress Wayne Pickering *and* punish Mr Bolton for giving me five hundred lines! My evil plan worked – Wayne never bullied me after that."

As they stood up to leave, Fred shook Hugo Gilby warmly by the hand, knowing this was an offer he couldn't refuse…

Hugo promised to lend Fred the money he needed, then step back, he'd be no more than a sleeping partner. The garden centre was merely an investment for his sons, Rupert and Piers.

Hugo looked surprised when asked if anyone had intended to build low maintenance bungalows on the site. He laughed, what a load of rubbish; bungalows had never been discussed. Who on earth suggested such nonsense? Rupert wanted the land for a garden centre, nothing else.

Fred decided to keep shtum; he'd no desire to get Alicia into trouble, call her a liar, or cause a row between husband and wife…

The following day, Fred had a long and productive conversation with Kenny Baker, owner of the local Cash and Carry warehouse. Kenny was looking forward to becoming the new owner of Dawson's corner shop. He'd found an excellent manager who was keen to grab the reins of *Kenny's Cash and Carry*. Kenny had no intention of selling his profitable warehouse. "Is it okay, Fred, if I change the shop's name?"

Fred laughed, "You can do whatever you like, Ken, it'll be your shop. Mind you, I wouldn't call it *Bakers,* no, you'll get customers coming in expecting nothing but bread and cakes!

"Don't you forget my old girls – especially Mrs Lovage. I said you'd carry on delivering their groceries: they were relieved, I can tell you."

Danny planned to work full-time at the garden centre but needed to remind his father, Saturdays were special – he'd still be working at Sanderson's Art Gallery. It was a good way to meet new, interesting people and so much more than a part-time job. "I wouldn't have it any other way, son," replied his dad, patting him on the back, "I know how much art means to you, so go ahead, do whatever makes you happy."

Jenny had been deep in thought. "Fred. Alicia's pecan pie was delicious, wasn't it? I shall ask her for the recipe. I can double-up and make an extra-large one, perfect for the café. *I'm so excited!* I can hardly believe it, at last, our dreams are about to come true."

Fred Dawson took a fresh pair of pyjamas from the bottom shelf of the airing cupboard, wondering if Jenny would be 'in the mood.' He smiled, perhaps I should get myself a pair of silk pyjamas; something sexier than stripes! He hoped she wouldn't turn over and face the window, otherwise, sleep would elude him. His head was full of bright ideas...

Jenny was in the bathroom, removing her make-up and brushing her teeth.

Fred's thoughts continued apace, recent events weighing heavily upon his mind. Rupert Gilby had been incredibly naïve, but we all make mistakes. It would have been extremely difficult to say *no* to the O'Reilly brothers, by all accounts they were aggressive and threatening. Poor Rupert, he'd no idea they were rogue traders, conmen and criminals!

Fred was nobody's fool: if he wanted to own a garden centre, then joining forces with the Gilby family seemed the sensible and only option. The future looked bright – for everyone.

Chapter 9

Spring 2001 - A Grand Opening

"Are you sure, love? *Alan Broadstone,* him off the telly, is going to open our garden centre? I don't believe it! What's in it for him?"

Danny laughed. "Don't be naïve, mum, he'll be charging us a flat fee of three thousand pounds which, to be honest, is quite reasonable. No-one does anything for free these days. Most of these so-called celebrities wouldn't turn up for less than ten grand. Alan's a decent bloke and he knows what he's talking about, he should, he presented Gardeners World for many years. We don't want some cheapo, third-rate comedian cutting the ribbon, do we? Alan's agent said they plan these things – they don't just make it up as they go along. Once he's cut the ribbon, they'll photograph him in your café, eating a slice of cake. You'd enjoy that, wouldn't you? He loves coffee and walnut, so be prepared! After he's eaten a slice of cake, he'll walk over to *Suzy's Fabulous Fashions* and pretend to buy something special for his wife, like a silk scarf. Don't worry, he's a pro, he's done it all before…

"He'll bring in the punters, yeah, he's got loads of fans, especially middle-aged ladies. D'you know something, mum? I'm fed-up with seeing that empty car park, I want to see it full! With any luck, the centre will be packed-out. Alan's agent will get us a spot on the local tv news, you know, at six-thirty. I'd better ring Rupert and let him know; I imagine Alicia and Hugo will want to meet Alan."

Danny chuckled. "I bet they'll try and get their faces on tv, although, Alicia might think that was 'vulgar.'

Fortunately, the Gilbys and the Dawsons had agreed on most things. Hugo and Rupert kept their word, standing back, letting Fred have his way. However, a few problems had arisen when designing the garden centre's prominent sign.

"What shall we call it then?" asked Hugo, "Gilby and Dawson, or the other way round?"

Fred looked surprised – he shook his head. "Neither, Hugo – give us a break! Look,

I'm sorry but it's not negotiable; the name of Gilby will *not* be appearing on any sign, merchandise or carrier bags; that would be a very bad move.

"The residents of Bexhill, Hastings and Eastbourne have long memories, they'll always associate the name of Gilby with asbestos. I'm afraid Rupert will just have to live with it and unfortunately, so will you! Oh, by the way, the logo will be a small, dark green cedar tree, designed by my son, and the tagline: *Dawson's Garden Centre. No-one beats our prices!*"

Rupert stretched and yawned noisily, looking like a spoilt child who's seeking attention. He'd heard more than enough about asbestos and the O'Reilly brothers. Why did everyone have to keep dragging it up?

Hugo glared at his son before replying. "Can I add a few words, please, Fred? I was thinking: *Everything for the garden and more!*"

Fred was in a good mood; everything was going to plan. "Yeah, alright Hugo, sounds good to me. We'll combine the two, shall we?"

Dawson's Garden Centre

Everything for the garden and more

No-one beats our prices

No more than a few wispy clouds moved slowly across the azure sky. Fred looked towards the car park, he nodded, it was beginning to fill up. The weather was on their side – Jenny felt sure this was a favourable sign on such an auspicious occasion. The Dawsons were excited, at last, Fred's long-held dream was about to come true…

Danny smiled, "Oh, hello there, Mrs Lovage, what a nice surprise. I bet you were first thorough the door this morning! Are you enjoying our grand opening?"

"Oh, yes, Danny, this place is amazing: it's like a little village – with a roof! For me, it's somewhere nice to visit when it's raining. The bus stops right outside, you know, well, what more could I want? I'm sure many other towns will follow your example and build one of these marvellous garden centres."

Elsie, feeling excited, had yet to finish her critique.

"By the way, the ladies' toilets are spotless and very smart. No doubt I was the first customer to use them." She giggled. "Does that mean I get a prize? Your mum put a vase of daffs in there, nice touch. Look, I treated myself to a pair of shoes from your Auntie Suzy's shop. Comfort comes first at my age, no more stiletto heels."

Danny smiled. Elsie was so sweet. "Right then, madam – would you care to meet Alan Broadstone?"

"Oh, yes please, he's my favourite, I love him to bits. I shall ask for his autograph…"

"Alan is outside admiring the camellias, a few of the flowers have opened up already, you'll be amazed, there are some fabulous colours…"

Jenny smiled, "Here's your pot of tea, Mrs Lovage, there's a warm cheese scone to go with it. Fred said you were his favourite customer, so it's on the house. Now listen, you mustn't worry, Kenny Baker will look after you and the other ladies – he'll carry on delivering your groceries, free of charge."

"Oh, thanks, that's a big weight off my mind. Guess who I've been chatting to? Alan Broadstone, off the telly, he gave me a hug, cheeky boy. My sister, Diana, will be green with envy. I wonder, can I ask you a favour, please?"

Jenny nodded. "Yes, of course you can."

"Well, my husband died three years ago and I get lonely, especially during the winter months when it gets dark so early. Can I come and work here, please, with you and your lovely family? I might be seventy-three, but I'm fighting fit. I'll wash-up, wipe the tables, sweep the floors, anything you like, apart from operating the tills. I'd get flustered; I don't like using those nasty debit and credit card machines: frightening things. No, I like cash – that's proper money."

Mrs Lovage looked wistful. "To be honest, I still miss pounds shillings and pence, and feet and inches. I still measure my cake ingredients in ounces. Those grams are far too small!"

Mrs Lovage was always making daft comments; no wonder people enjoyed spending time with her. How could Jenny possibly say no?

"Yes, of course you can, Elsie, you can help me out; I'd be most grateful. I'd no idea we'd be so busy, not that I'm complaining. How about afternoons, when we've finished doing hot food like toasted sandwiches and soup? There's always lots of clearing up to do. Shall we say – three 'til five? I know the bus stops outside, but if it's raining, we'll give you a lift home, it's not far. You can start when you like and I'll pay you the same rate as all the other ladies."

Thanks to Alan's highly successful visit, a five-minute spot on local tv and the front page of both the *Bexhill Observer* and the *Eastbourne Gazette,* tills had been ringing. Fred had made a rough calculation but he was way off mark; takings were twice as much as he'd anticipated. Perhaps this would be considered a perfectly normal outcome for 'week one' of any similar enterprise. The Dawsons were delighted: there'd been hundreds of curious customers and a great deal of impulse buying.

Auntie Suzy would need to re-stock; she'd sold more clothing in one weekend than she'd sold from her small shop, in the town centre, during the previous month!

Having a Grand Opening in late spring had always been Fred's intention. People were out and about spending their hard-earned cash and hoping for warm sunny days. They were enthusiastic and eager to treat themselves to flowering shrubs, perennial plants, garden furniture, pergolas and anything else that might improve or beautify their gardens…

Jenny still had a few negative thoughts; perhaps, after the initial excitement, the public would lose interest and she'd be left with unwanted cakes or saucepans filled to the brim with home-made vegetable soup! Fortunately, the reverse happened and an orderly queue formed, every day, from eleven o'clock until they stopped serving hot food at three. Jenny named her café, *Tasty Treats.* Two ladies had been interviewed, both would be joining the team, helping to lighten the load.

Fred Dawson had been right to follow his dream – garden centres *were* the future…

At the beginning of May (as he was paying for his diesel at the BP garage) Danny's eyes were drawn to an interesting article halfway down the front page of the Daily Express. The stark headline was certainly eye-catching: *The brothers from Hell!* Although the word asbestos sent shivers down his spine, he felt compelled to purchase a copy. The O'Reilly brothers had made yet another court appearance; they'd been photographed (by a passing motorist's passenger) dumping furniture and other household rubbish in a country lane, just outside Maidenhead, Berkshire. They'd been fined eight thousand pounds, far less than before, as no asbestos was discovered. Patrick had smirked and given a thumbs-up to the magistrate when a sentence of six months imprisonment, suspended for two years, was also handed out. Hardly a deterrent…

After sentencing, their surname was mentioned, by a stern-faced magistrate, in connection with another similar crime, the illegal dumping of rubbish, including a vast amount of highly toxic asbestos. On this previous occasion, the O'Reilly brothers had driven over a hundred miles in order to carry out the despicable act of fly-tipping. The items had been removed from a land clearance site in Bexhill-on-sea, East Sussex. Their pre-planned destination was the beautiful and previously unspoilt Cotswold village of Lower Foxton…

Danny's heart rate increased: he'd no idea the brothers had been traced; Rupert hadn't said a word. He must have been persuaded, by the Thames Valley Police, to hand over their details. Danny shook his head – um, was that wise?

A photograph of the O'Reilly brothers, leaving court, would make any witness think twice before testifying. These two seasoned criminals were best avoided, they had long memories; even the police gave them a wide berth.

No doubt the brothers would feel obliged to revive their favourite scam, *tarmac,* always a nice little earner. In their opinion, the English were a foolish race: too polite, indecisive and unable to say *No thanks!* Sometimes, they were able to con two or three couples in one day!

Step 1: Find a nice quiet area; bungalows preferably. Bungalows supply friendly, gullible, elderly couples. Knock on a few doors, smile broadly...

Ask the elderly householder (with a tarmac drive) if he would like a top-quality covering put over his old tarmac. As luck would have it, you have some tarmac left over from a previous job, it needs to be put down immediately before it hardens. It's a one off, a bargain at five hundred pounds.

Step 2: You look worried: oh, dear, bad news. On taking a closer look, you discovered several fine cracks in their tarmac drive, however, you'd need good eyesight to spot them. If the householder is wearing spectacles, so much the better. Remedial action must be taken immediately before more cracks appear and weeds start to take hold. The homeowner is at first confused, then worried and practically begs you to re-tarmac his drive.

Step 3: A thin layer of poor-quality tarmac is spread over the driveway, leaving it messy and bumpy. Sometimes the tarmac finds its way onto cherished ornaments, flower beds and brickwork.

When the job's finished you become angry, you raise your voice, telling the homeowners they must be confused. The amount due is five *thousand* pounds. Then, with an air of menace and a crowbar in your hand, you make a suggestion…

As most sensible people don't keep vast amounts of money in their home, you offer to drive the victim(s), pale-faced and terrified, to the bank or building society, whereupon a very large cash withdrawal is made. Occasionally, this crime is reported to the police, but most people realise how stupid they've been, how naïve, and prefer to draw a line under the whole sorry episode…

The scam provided the brothers with endless bundles of cash which they kept in old biscuit tins under the floorboards. All they needed was a flatbed truck and some tarmac. They kept to the Midlands and south of England, always making a careful note of the towns and villages where they'd been successful – after all, they didn't wish to visit anywhere twice!

Letters from the tax office were ignored and rarely followed up. It was rumoured, if you went to see the O'Reilly brothers you might not get out alive, you'd be murdered and fed to the pigs. Although this suggestion seemed way over the top, no member of staff was prepared to 'give it a go.' The brothers, now in their early forties, were a law unto themselves, neither man had ever paid a penny in tax or national insurance.

For them, life was a breeze.

Joseph and Patrick had been born and brought up in County Wexford, Southern Ireland. After moving to England, they purchased a smallholding where they kept a few ponies, pigs and chickens, all of whom were treated badly.

O'Reilly's fresh brown eggs were popular but expensive; they were sold by local shops as *organic*. Nothing could be further from the truth. No shop owner was brave enough to visit the smallholding to check out the living conditions and type of feed given to the poor old hens. If the brothers said the eggs were organic, so be it, no-one would dream of challenging them. Besides, a huge guard dog, with a certain reputation and the name of *Killer*, kept visitors to a minimum.

There was brave and there was downright stupid!

Chapter 10

Fred is left feeling guilty...

"Oh, Elsie, before you go – would you like a couple of these penstemons? They're looking a bit straggly, they ought to be in the ground by now. I'll trim the others back and take fifty per cent off the price."

"Yes, I would, cheers, Fred. I'll take a *Garnet* and an *Apple Blossom.*" Elsie nodded, "They'll look very pretty together, one deep red and one pink and white."

Fred sighed. "I shall have to move those trays of purple and white pansies, it's too hot for them over by the wall. I'll find a bit of shade, somewhere. If you'd like to wait, I'll give you a lift home."

"No, no, you carry on, love, my bus will be here in less than ten minutes. I'll come in early tomorrow, if you like – dead-head the pansies and give 'em all a good soaking."

Fred smiled warmly. "Please do, Elsie, that would be very helpful. Fortunately, they're still damp from that heavy shower we had lunch time. Right then, I'll see you tomorrow."

Mrs Lovage was the only person waiting at the bus stop. She waved as a grey-haired gentleman hurried along on the other side of the road. He recognised her from the café, smiled, then waved back. Such a sweet lady, I think her name is Elsie. If I'd been in the car, I could have stopped and given her a lift. Don't get your hopes up, Thomas Evans; she's got a pretty face and a lively personality – a lady like that is bound to have a man in her life. Suddenly, a feeling of intense loneliness overwhelmed him…

Elsie watched, fascinated, as the man continued walking towards the library and a row of small independent shops.

Next time he comes in for a cuppa and a cheese scone, I shall make a point of talking to him. She smiled to herself. He's rather attractive, about my age too – always seems to be on his own. If he asked me for a date, would I say yes? Course I would! Perhaps I should make the first move and invite him round for

Sunday lunch, that is, if he doesn't have a partner. I think most men, living alone, would appreciate a roast dinner.

A noisy, dark blue transit van, stinking of diesel, came to a sudden halt – the passenger door slid open. A scruffy individual, wearing a grey hoodie and jeans, leapt out, and tried to grab hold of Elsie. Without thinking, she poked him quite viciously in his left eye.

"Ahh, get off me you bitch!" he screamed.

A few seconds later the bus arrived. The man panicked and jumped back inside the van. With a screech of tyres and a cloud of black smoke the van shot off in the direction of Bexhill town centre. The bus driver, seeing the commotion, ran to Elsie's side.

She was shaken up, but insisted, "I'm okay, don't fuss. My late husband was in the army, he taught me a few handy moves. If you get attacked, always try to poke the assailant in the eye, it'll stop him, immediately. I hope my husband is looking down – he'd be so proud of me."

The young bus driver was impressed by the elderly lady's bravery. He put his arm around her waist, "Come with me, madam, let's get you inside the bus."

A teenage girl, wearing a school uniform smiled at Elsie. "Come and sit next to me. Fancy a wine gum?"

Elsie, cool as a cucumber, replied, "To be honest, love, I'd rather have a *glass* of wine! Will someone pick up my penstemons, please? They're over there, look, by the bus stop – lying on the pavement. That idiot must have knocked them over."

When the transit van sped away, the bus driver had tried to read the number plate but he couldn't, it had been smeared with mud. He was unable to decipher a single letter or number…

Elsie's frightening encounter was reported to the police, but without a number plate, it would be impossible to trace the vehicle; nevertheless, they would record the crime and send someone along to take a statement.

No-one, apart from Elsie, heard the man's voice. After a few moments of contemplation, she said he sounded 'a bit like a foreigner' although he might have been Scottish or even Welsh. "Sorry, I'm no good with accents, never have been. He was very smelly – I do remember that! Yes, stale sweat, onions, cigarettes and diesel." She laughed. "I have an excellent sense of smell, don't you agree?"

The following morning, just as the café was opening up, a young woman arrived, wearing a grey trouser suit and a pale blue and white stripy blouse. Newly promoted D.S. Sophie Hollis, from Bexhill C.I.D., had an appointment with Mrs Lovage, who'd asked her to *'Please come in early, get it over with, then I won't have to think about it ever again…"*

The young detective couldn't help but admire Mrs Lovage: a remarkable lady who didn't seem unduly upset by her frightening and rather bizarre ordeal. Many ladies (of any age) would have become hysterical and taken days to recover…

The café was quiet: few customers came in before ten-thirty. Sophie was invited, by the manageress, to join them at one of the tables. Jenny smiled at the young detective. "I know it's early but would you care to join us for a coffee and a slice of lemon drizzle cake? On the house?"

Like any self-respecting woman, Sophie nodded. "Oh, yes please. I skipped breakfast this morning so I'm really hungry. Thank you."

After taking Elsie's statement, Sophie stayed for a while, treating herself to a second latte. Mrs Dawson was a talented lady; great coffee, moist cake. Whilst I'm here, she thought, I may as well have a look round, I'm in no hurry to get back to the office, last month's crime figures can cope without me! She was pleasantly surprised by the variety of items on offer. As Dawson's tagline professed: *'Everything for the garden and more!'*

Sophie's mother loved orchids: there were two in the hallway and even with minimum attention, they flourished.

Sophie stopped abruptly; one orchid in particular caught her eye – she'd never seen anything quite so beautiful. It looked as if some unknown but talented artist had added sploshes of magenta, pale mauve and tangerine to a white background. She counted thirteen flowers and nearly as many buds. The following Thursday would be her mum's birthday and the first she'd faced since the untimely death of Sophie's father.

The orchid was in a glazed white pot; anything else would have detracted from its striking colours. Sophie grabbed hold of the pot, even though no other customers were within four metres. She decided not to spoil the moment by looking at the price, well, not until she reached the till…

Sophie lived at home which wasn't unusual for a young lady who wished to follow a demanding career. After a depressing day dealing with drug-addicts, shop-lifters and worse, it was good to get home to a welcoming smile and one of her mum's tasty meals. Sadly, getting on the property ladder seemed no more than a pipe dream. Her mum offered to help with the deposit, but even with her kindness and support, she wouldn't be in a position to buy a house for many years. Besides, since the death of her beloved father, money was tight…

That evening, after the six o'clock news, Jenny turned off the television. "Are you alright, Fred? You seem quiet this evening. Fancy another glass of wine?"

Fred didn't wish to be awkward, but Jenny knew only too well why he wasn't in a chatty mood. He'd hardly slept a wink since Elsie was man-handled by a complete stranger! Who on earth would wish her harm? No sane person, surely, yet a youngish man had tried to drag her into his van. It was like a scene from a tv drama where someone famous or wealthy is kidnapped. He shook his head. No disrespect to Elsie, but it's usually schoolgirls (perish the thought) or attractive young ladies who are dragged off the streets, not ladies of pensionable age.

Elsie had been standing at the bus stop wearing her pale green tabard. This item of clothing displayed Dawson's cedar tree logo –

an indication of where she worked. Might there be a connection somewhere?

Fred finished his second glass of Merlot. If only he'd insisted on driving Elsie home. If he had, the bizarre and somewhat disturbing incident would not have occurred. He felt guilty; the blood rushed to his cheeks. Those flippin' purple and white pansies could have remained where they were, by the wall, for another forty minutes…

Elsie was popular with the customers: she rarely went home at five and nothing was too much trouble. Jenny had said, the previous week, *'Elsie is a little diamond, what would we do without her?'*

"It's a mystery to me, Jen, it sends shivers down your spine. You hear of such awful things these days. Let's not forget, there were two men in that van. If he'd tried to grab her handbag, yes, that would make sense, but it was clearly *Elsie* he was after. The mind boggles. Perhaps we'll never know the reason. I wonder – did the men mistake Elsie for somebody else?"

"Well, it's a possibility, Fred. That went through my mind as well. Perhaps there's a lady who looks like our Elsie and she's reported them to the police. They spotted her, quite by chance, at the bus stop and wanted to punish her!"

Fred looked shocked. "Oh, my God, they might be the sort of tradesmen who demand money first, then build you a dodgy extension, or the type who put in a gas-boilers when they're not qualified."

Fred looked embarrassed. "You might think I'm going crazy but sometimes I wonder if the garden centre is cursed."

Jenny squeezed her husband's hand. "Cursed? Isn't that a bit dramatic? Whatever makes you think that?"

"Well, Danny spotted the perfect site, just what we were looking for, and everything was going according to plan, wasn't it? That is, until I had the medical and Doctor Patel discovered my sky-high cholesterol. After that, no-one would give me a mortgage.

"We were convinced, weren't we? Being Danny's friend *and* a merchant banker, Rupert would be more than happy to help us – we'd only have to sign on the dotted line. Instead, along with that damn boss of his, David Fanshawe, he stole my dream: that's unforgivable…

"Still, the Gilby family saw sense, eventually, they had to, after the asbestos fiasco. Things have worked out well for us, so I shouldn't be downcast. Do you know something? At this rate, I shall be paying off Hugo Gilby in no time at all.

"Of course, Elsie being grabbed like that, well, it puts a dampener on everything. I suppose we ought to look on the bright side, she fought back and physically, no harm done. She's been so brave. I hope it's genuine and she doesn't suffer flash-backs in the future."

"Oh dear, let's not even go there, Fred. Of one thing I'm sure, Elsie will never have to wait at that bus stop again. If necessary, we'll write down a few names – members of staff who finish at five and are willing to drive her home to Windermere Gardens.

"Coming to work on the bus won't be a problem, no nasty memories. Elsie uses the pelican crossing, then comes straight into the main building. Don't worry, she'll be fine."

Chapter 11

An intriguing Saturday morning

As Danny turned the corner into Seaview Parade, he noticed a scruffy individual, leaning forward, peering through the windows of the art gallery. The man moved towards him, watching closely as Danny fumbled with the complicated lock on the shiny, black, replacement door.

He poked Danny's chest with a grubby finger. His voice, loud but slurred, suggested he'd been drinking alcohol despite the early hour.

"I'm looking for a mate; Spike Henson. He owes me money. D'you know him?"

Danny shook his head and mouthed 'no.'

The man looked at him, suspiciously. "He lives in Pevensey Terrace, it's round here somewhere – you sure you don't know 'im? Well, how do I get there? Oh, I need a couple of quid, for a cuppa."

The man was in a jumpy mood, firing questions without waiting for answers. Danny's assumptions were correct – the man was under the influence of more than just alcohol. Danny felt vulnerable. A young bull terrier accompanied the man, it looked frightened and undernourished. A length of knotted string was tied to its collar. After giving directions to Pevensey Terrace, Danny said, "Hang on a minute." He hurried inside the gallery and opened the top drawer of his desk. He grabbed a packet of custard creams which he handed over, along with a five-pound note. He hoped the stranger would share the biscuits with his dog. The man nodded, lit a roll-up then shuffled away…

It had been an unusually quiet morning, only two customers, neither of whom turned out to be big spenders. The lady from Berkshire, staying in Eastbourne for the week, bought a large paper-weight for her husband's birthday. She'd been looking for something attractive to put on his much-loved oak desk. She'd selected a classic design made from opaque glass with a scorpion etched on the top.

"It's his birth sign, he'll love it. It has a look of Lalique about it, don't you think?"

Danny agreed, of course...

At ten-fifteen, an elderly lady purchased a box of blank greetings cards, suitable for any occasion. An excellent choice, Monet's water lilies. During his time at Norwich University, Danny studied Monet's work, together with other less well-known French impressionist painters.

The artist made over two hundred and fifty paintings of his favourite flowers – water lilies.

The lady seemed in no hurry to leave, preferring to engage Danny in conversation. She examined a few items, nodding with approval.

"I love this gallery. Mrs Sanderson has worked wonders. I used to walk past without a second thought, but now you've branched out and decided to sell all these delightful things – not just paintings – well, I was lured in. Your range of glassware is superb and who can resist a Moorcroft vase or stemmed ginger jar?"

"Thank you. I'll pass on your comments to Mrs Sanderson."

The lady smiled. "I keep a few blank cards and some stamps in the sideboard drawer. At my age it's easy to forget birthdays. If my card arrives late, no-one minds, I have a certain reputation for putting a fifty-pound note inside."

Danny looked wide-eyed. "You must be very popular with family and friends. You can send me a belated birthday card any time you like!"

The lady checked her watch then left, promising to call in again for another chat. I hope she does, thought Danny, she's quite a character.

At eleven-thirty, Danny turned the sign to *closed* and nipped out for a coffee. Sanderson's Art Gallery was in a row of privately owned shops, each with its own personality. *Café Bruno* had a reputation for making first class coffee.

After grabbing a packet of crisps and a newspaper from the Minimart, he stopped to chat with the owner, Jasmina Khan, about the arrest of a local businessman who'd murdered his wife and buried her in the garden. Jasmina shivered, but laughed when Danny changed the subject.

"These organic cheese and onion crisps are quite potent, I bought some last week. If anyone comes into the gallery, after I've eaten them, I must avoid breathing in their direction." He laughed. "There's always a packet of extra strong mints in the top drawer – just in case.

Danny had been in the stock room when *she* arrived…

A delicate blue and white porcelain vase (a special order) needed to be wrapped with great care, it was being collected later in the day. He'd been looking for sheets of tissue paper and a fresh roll of bubble wrap when the doorbell rang, he hurried back to the showroom.

Standing in front of an abstract oil painting was a sight that made his heart beat faster: the enchanting, Roxanne Elliott-Boyd.

The weather was thundery and oppressive. Roxy wore a strapless cotton dress – pale green, pink and turquoise, a random pattern on a white background. Her long blonde hair enhanced the bright colours that on someone less attractive may have looked garish. As she bent forward to examine a dainty piece of pottery, Danny had to look away, she wasn't wearing a bra. Was he correct in thinking she'd planned this manoeuvre in order to get a reaction? If so, why? Roxy smiled, then gave him a friendly hug. He could feel the warmth of her skin against his neck. He could smell her perfume, light yet fruity, it reminded him of apple blossom.

Roxy put her hands on Danny's waist and pulled him roughly towards her. To his surprise, she pressed her body firmly against his…

His cheeks felt hot, were they pink? She held onto him for longer than expected. He didn't care, he was happy to stay exactly where he was, in her arms, until she let him go. She stood back, then looked at him, flirtatiously.

"Oh, Danny, that was nice, well, more than nice – for me anyway. You know how I feel about you, don't you?"

Danny didn't know what to say or how to react. Please don't flirt with me, he thought, it's cruel – you're Rupert's fiancée! The telephone rang, if not, would Roxy have kissed him? Possibly – no, definitely…

It was Mrs Greenberg, calling about her blue and white vase. She'd had a fall, fractured a bone in her wrist and couldn't drive. Would Danny be kind enough to deliver it? He said he'd be delighted, he'd call round after work, between five and six.

Roxy gazed out of the window, watching customers as they parked outside the coffee shop or walked further down the road towards the post office and the Minimart.

She turned and spoke to Danny in a business-like manner; it was as if their sexually-charged embrace had never happened and he was no more than a casual acquaintance. Did Roxanne behave in this way towards all her male friends? Was she no more than a tease, testing the water, wondering how he would react?

"I'm here because my cousin, Olivia Barclay, is getting married next month. You may have seen her in Vogue or Cosmopolitan. She's a model too, we're always bumping into one another. Olivia is only five years' older than me but she fears her career is coming to an end. Isn't it awful? Over the hill at thirty-two! Gorgeous girl, great fun.

"Olivia and her fiancé, Harry Worthington, are renovating a stone cottage in Dorset. It's just a small, week-end place, 18th century. They'll need something colourful to brighten up all those dark oak beams, but nothing modern…

"Over there, next to the staircase, that's just the sort of thing I'm looking for."

Roxy paused, deep in thought, then moved closer to examine the painting. "It's delightful, nothing too fussy. A bowl filled with deep red cherries – the colour is exquisite – plus an art deco vase with a single peachy-coloured Damask rose. Olivia will love it. Look how the light catches the side of the cut-glass bowl, how clever, such a talented artist. Oh, darling, that's amazing – it's by Celia Fenton, I am impressed. I've heard good things about her. She's one to watch. How much is it?"

Danny raised his eyebrows, "If it's by Celia Fenton then it's going to be pricey, I can promise you that."

He opened a small black notebook. "Ah, here it is. It's called, *'Arrangement in crimson and amber.'* A rather uninspiring title. It came in just a few weeks ago, there's been a lot of interest. It's priced at £4,800."

Roxy smiled. "That's okay, sweetie, who cares? Daddy's paying – after all, it is a family wedding. *Yes, I'll take it."*

She paused, then moved closer in order to stroke the hair at the back of Danny's neck. "No, better still," she whispered, "I want *you* to deliver it."

Roxy smiled and gave him a look that could only mean one thing. Danny caught his breath. Was Roxy inviting him to her home, hoping he'd make love to her? Don't kid yourself, he thought, she's just a tease.

"Right then, Mr Dawson, now the present has been chosen, will you open that packet of crisps? I'm so hungry. As you know, we models eat practically nothing." She laughed, "I don't know how we survive."

They sat together on the faded leather sofa, positioned at the rear of the gallery from where the paintings could best be enjoyed. They talked about everything under the sun, including the disgraceful way the Dawsons had been treated by Rupert and his boss, David Fanshawe. When their plans went horribly wrong, Hugo and Rupert were obliged to put out the hand of friendship in order to mask Rupert's crass behaviour.

"They thought we didn't matter; we were just the *little* people who could be cast aside," remarked Danny, with anger in his voice. "They stole my dad's dream and nearly broke his heart."

Roxy sighed. "Rupert learned his lesson though, didn't he? That nasty business with the O'Reilly brothers and the asbestos, I could hardly believe it – Rupert was such an idiot –

talk about Mr Gullible. I don't know what possessed him to employ them; I suppose they were cheap. He's lucky, how kind of Hugo to pay off his debts – not many fathers would do that."

Danny shrugged. "He only did it to avoid further scandal. The brothers have been in court again, yep, dumping stuff outside Maidenhead, a place called Furze Platt. There was a big article about them in the Daily Telegraph. A smaller fine this time, but with the addition of a suspended sentence. It's ridiculous, they should be in prison. The headline was '*The brothers from Hell.*' Spot on. They prey on old-age pensioners and have a reputation for threatening anyone who refuses to pay their extortionate charges. I hope they never come back to this neck of the woods. Rupert shouldn't have grassed them up though, they are dangerous, with a capital D!"

Roxy laughed. "Oh, hark at you, '*grassed them up*' you sound like a criminal!"

Chapter 12

An unexpected by-election

The sordid details revealed by the sudden death of Peter Desmond-Brown caused quite a stir in government circles but provided hours of amusement for the general public...

His face appeared on the front page of every newspaper and countless television news-bulletins. Peter had become famous for saying: *'This country has become a cess-pit; there's too much interest in sex. We must return to Christian values: clean living, marriage and sobriety.'*

This outspoken and deeply religious Member of Parliament had died in bed, from a massive heart attack. Unfortunately, Peter was lying next to his bi-sexual lover, a twenty-year-old drag queen with the stage-name of *Sparkle*.

According to Sparkle's best friend (who wished to remain anonymous) Peter was stark naked apart from a bright pink feather boa. 'Oh, yes,' added the friend, 'silly me, I nearly forgot,

Peter was wearing a lovely pair of diamond earrings.'

It was the beginning of May, 2012. People were, in general, more broad-minded and tolerant than they had once been, but nevertheless, for the Daily Mirror and the Daily Express, sales doubled. Who doesn't love a scandal? Especially when a self-righteous, hypocritical politician is involved…

Fifty-seven-year-old Peter, a God-fearing Christian and devoted family man, had made a point of being photographed with his children. Aubrey and Benedict (both in their twenties) and thirteen-year-old twins, Melissa and Hermione, knew, if they expected money from their father, they must smile and look happy in front of the cameras. Striding out to church on Sunday mornings, with his beloved wife Camilla, Peter had expected and received warm handshakes from his loyal constituents.

The Conservative party was in a state of panic. Replacing this unpopular M.P. was going to be challenging: next time, they must have a more rigorous selection process. The small constituency of Bexhill and Pevensey Bay contained several thousand retirees, many of whom were demanding a less *kinky* Member of Parliament, someone they could trust, otherwise they would be 'lending their votes' to the Liberal Democrats. Rupert's name was put forward by his father and more importantly, by Uncle James, a well-respected magistrate who, despite being in his sixties, was still a very handsome man. Just like Rupert (his nephew) Uncle James had inherited the Gilby genes, making them both irresistible to women.

The only fly in the ointment seemed to be the 'asbestos fiasco' a light-hearted name given to a shocking and never to be forgotten episode in Rupert's life. Uncle James laughed at them, saying, 'For goodness-sake don't fuss, it'll be no more than a glitch.' Once they'd spread a few ugly rumours about the Dawson family, all would be forgiven.

Thirty-seven-year-old Rupert Gilby would be ideal, but had he considered the demands of a political career?

His wife, the beautiful model, Roxanne Elliott-Boyd, had no intention of selling her Mayfair home, which was an added bonus. Every M.P. needs an apartment in the capital. Roxy was seen as the quintessential English rose: trustworthy, intelligent and once seen, never forgotten. She would be a real asset to the Conservative party. Together, the Gilbys made a delightful couple – heads would turn – yet another box ticked in Rupert's favour.

One kindly Labour M.P., a man in his mid-seventies, said Rupert and Roxy reminded him of the 1960s. A new era, and a time when it seemed the whole world had fallen in love with John F Kennedy and his beautiful wife, Jacqueline...

A few of Hugo's friends (at the Masonic Lodge) were a little concerned, Rupert had no political experience whatsoever. However, once Hugo made a few helpful suggestions regarding stocks and shares and where to invest their money, they soon came to the conclusion, yes, of course, Rupert was just the man for the job.

Once the by-election had taken place, Hugo and Alicia organized a party for Rupert: he deserved nothing less. Being elected as the new Member of Parliament for Bexhill and Pevensey Bay (albeit with a slightly reduced majority) was quite an achievement.

Much to their surprise, the Dawsons received an invitation to the party. Jenny sighed, "Oh, dear, I suppose we ought to go."

Fred raised an eyebrow. "Huh, I know what you mean. I don't want to go either, but we must keep them sweet, after all they've done what they promised – kept out of my way at the garden centre and left me to get on with things. Everything's ticking over nicely, profits have increased, year on year, that's all one can hope for."

Rupert was feeling buoyant, his maiden speech, made the previous Thursday, had been a great success.

Afterwards, in the House of Commons tea room, the Prime Minister, David Cameron, had shaken him by the hand and patted him on the back! Rupert had been advised to talk about something *safe,* a subject with which party members and the majority of the British public would readily agree.

The environment had been suggested, yes, definitely, *green issues.* More to the point, after the asbestos fiasco, it would be a good choice, he must show how caring and how environmentally sound he was.

Ever since the thwarted kidnapping of Elsie Lovage, Danny and D.S. Sophie Hollis had become good friends. It was hard to believe it was nearly eleven years since this bizarre and worrying incident had taken place. Sophie hinted at marriage or perhaps living together. Danny was fond of Sophie and he found her attractive, but he didn't love her and he never would. He wished very much that he did, it would make life so much easier. His parents didn't help either, they thought Sophie was wonderful and they were hoping for grand-children.

The party was in full-flow with guests sitting outside on the newly constructed patio, hoping the insects wouldn't bite. The 15th July was also Roxy's birthday – another reason to feel joyful. The lights inside the house had been dimmed and candles lit. Danny was dancing with Sophie; a slow, romantic melody played in the background.

"I'm going to sit the next one out, Danny, I'm exhausted, I've had one hell of a day."

"That's okay," he replied, "No probs. I shall take a walk round the garden, it's cooler outside."

The Gilby's close neighbours and half the neighbourhood had been invited to the party, so there was no need to turn down the music. As Danny reached the top of the garden, behind the beech hedge and the shed, he sensed someone was following him. He stopped and looked over his shoulder: it was Roxy, a shiver ran down his spine. As she walked beneath a row of tiny fairy lights, her long blonde hair shimmered, as if made from spun gold. The patio doors were open wide. 'Lady in Red' could be heard, at full volume, it received a mixed reception. Some people thought it was no more than a slushy love song but for others, it brought back a host of meaningful memories.

"When was this popular?" asked Roxy.

Danny shrugged, "Mid-eighties, I think. I suppose it's spot-on if you fancy a slow dance."

Roxy smiled and beckoned him with one finger. *"Come here, Danny Dawson – dance with me, hold me close. I've missed you so much."*

Danny looked confused. *"You've missed me?* How can that be? I mean nothing to you…"

"You know that's not true. That Saturday, in the art gallery – *there was such a spark between us.* I knew, even then, I was falling in love with you. Then, like a fool, I married Rupert. I was in too deep, everything was arranged, I couldn't see a way out."

It was pointless trying to deny it, they were bewitched, besotted – head over heels in love.

The moment the music stopped, someone inside the house shouted, "Put it on again, Hugo, I'm on a promise tonight!"

After much laughter, a man, who sounded tipsy, replied, "Well who's a lucky boy then?" Once again, Chris de Burgh's unmistakable voice sailed to the top of the garden. It was a beautiful evening and for two people, the rest of the world didn't exist. Roxy pulled Danny towards her, then kissed him, longingly. They neither knew nor cared if anyone was watching.

Just after midnight, a taxi arrived, *"I'm here for the Dawsons,"* shouted the driver. Fred sat in the front, Sophie in the back, with Jenny and Danny. Fred looked over his shoulder; "You alright Sophie? You're very quiet. Hardly seen you all evening. We had a good time, didn't we, Jenny? Yeah – caught up with a few friends we hadn't seen for ages. Although, to be honest, I might have over-indulged in the old red wine department."

Sophie didn't feel obliged to join in or look cheerful. "I had a bad day at work, Fred, that's all. A young girl was mugged, she was terrified. Please ignore me, I'm just over-tired."

"Okay, we'd best drop you off first then. You'll be fine after a good night's sleep. Your job comes with a great deal of responsibility – the boss must have faith in you. Ah, here we are, Willow Drive, door to door. Goodnight Sophie, sleep well, love."

As the taxi pulled away, Jenny turned to Danny. "Have you two had a row? You could have cut the atmosphere with a knife…"

Danny raised his voice. "Look, *mother,* Sophie said she was tired, alright? Leave it – it's none of your damn business!"

The moment Danny was alone, he checked his phone, one text, great – it must be from Roxy. He tutted. No, it was from Sophie.

'I was in Gilby's garden looking for you when the full moon appeared. I saw you, kissing Roxy. I think you've always been in love with her. I won't play second fiddle to anyone. I promise I won't tell Rupert. Please, Danny, don't ever contact me again.'

Chapter 13

London and Paris

Danny's train left Eastbourne at eight-fifteen on Friday evening: thirty-five minutes late. Staff shortages, apparently. He ought to send a text to Roxy, just to let her know he was running late. It didn't matter, after all, they intended to spend the whole week-end together. He smiled, much of the time in bed, if I'm lucky...

Taking a taxi to Mayfair seemed the sensible option. Danny wasn't familiar with the underground system, he found it unnerving, especially the steep escalators. He felt anxious, which was unnecessary, nothing could go wrong. Rupert was abroad, doing what came naturally, charming people and drumming up business.

Rupert Gilby had no intention of 'giving up the day job' not with a salary of just under one million pounds.

Like most MPs, he tried to juggle more than one career – the result being, many of his constituents felt abandoned. Sometimes, replies to their letters (often begging for help) or friendly emails, offering support, received no more than a cursory acknowledgement.

Rupert was staying in Paris for the week, eyeing up another golden opportunity, although this time, in a less sought-after location than the Champs Elysees. Fanshawe and Peabody had been invited to bankroll a development of luxury apartments. Although this once admired Art Deco hotel had seen better days, it was still referred to as *Le Dauphin.* As the building had been empty for decades, the cost of refurbishment would be sky-high; everything from plumbing and re-wiring to a new damp course and underfloor central heating. All worked carried out must retain the Art Deco style thus adding to the developer's costs and the need for an 'eye-watering' loan from Fanshawe and Peabody. A financial arrangement of this magnitude made Rupert and his boss very, very, happy…

Chances like this came along once in a lifetime. They'd been fortunate, not *one* but *two* multi-million-pound developments in the heart of Paris. Rupert smiled and looked up to the sky.

"Somebody up there loves me! Oh, yes!"

Rupert managed to persuade his boss that it would be beneficial to the company if Desiree Marlow, his secretary, were to accompany him. Roxy would never find out, not unless some spineless, mischief-making individual decided to tell her! Desiree was bright, willing to work long hours and hoping for promotion. Her eyes were big, beautiful and the colour of plain chocolate; her completion – flawless. From the moment they were introduced, Rupert knew, very soon, he'd be making love to her. Would this be the golden opportunity he'd been waiting for?

A five-star double room (with access to swimming pool and gym) had been booked at the *Hotel de Paris,* for six nights. Asking Desiree if she would prefer a single room hadn't occurred to Rupert. Desiree was excited, she'd never been to Paris and more to the point, she'd fallen madly in love with her boss. She'd telephoned her mother (back home in Jamaica) and told her Rupert Gilby was the most attractive man she'd ever seen: just like a movie star. Her mother was furious and raised her voice.

"You behave yourself, my girl, he's a married man and a member of parliament, he'll be selfish, over-sexed and have a big ego. You are only twenty-two, darlin' – with your whole life before you. Watch out or he will destroy you."

As her mother continued with her unwelcome advice, Desiree flicked through a fashion magazine, paying little attention to her mother's stern words…

"I didn't scrimp and save and send you to a fancy secretarial school just to see you behave like a tart. Besides, sex before marriage is a sin; the good Lord sees all you do. If you don't believe me, you should read one of the sermons written by the Reverend Nathaniel Brookes. I'll send you a copy with my next email. On Sunday, after church, I shall ask him to pray for your soul and cast out the devil."

Desiree yawned, then giggled. "Mum, I love you very much, but please, lighten up! You are still living in the Victorian era – *there is no devil.*"

Letitia Marlow would have been shocked, had she known her precious daughter was taking the contraceptive pill, and had been doing so since falling in love with Rupert Gilby. Desiree was a virgin – but for how much longer?

Shane Marlow, Desiree's brother, had inherited his father's lack of commitment. Both men refused to get involved with their children's upbringing.

Desiree's father, Trenton, a local poet and artist, was an adulterer and a compulsive gambler. He'd fathered a number of children, scattered across Jamaica. He provided for none of them or even acknowledged their existence. Letitia had all but given up on her menfolk; why couldn't they be faithful? Jamaican men were too laid back about everything. Perhaps it was the tropical weather, or perhaps, too much marijuana.

Moving to London hadn't changed Shane's attitude to women; his girlfriend had a young baby, but so did his wife. Despite his casual attitude towards fatherhood, Desiree trusted her brother – she knew, in a crisis, he would be her rock. Woe-betide any man who upset his beautiful sister!

Desiree was an ambitious young lady prepared to work hard, sit exams and make a better life for herself. She rented a small flat, in Pimlico, with her cousin, Rosina, a legal secretary. After a few glasses of sauvignon blanc, the ladies made a vow, no man would be permitted to interfere with their chosen careers. Rosina was engaged to a solicitor, but Desiree was beginning a relationship that was bound to fail.

The last thing she needed was an affair with a married man, especially a vain and devious man with a reputation for chasing women…

Chapter 14

A despicable act

On the fifteenth of April, in rural Hampshire, an intelligent but somewhat naïve man made a decision that would cause untold misery and heartache for his beloved wife and family…

He signalled left, then turned off the main road; it was a mile and a quarter to Glebe Farm. He sighed. Two posties were off sick with some obscure tummy bug: thank goodness it was Friday. *Paint it Black*, by the Rolling Stones, was belting out at full volume. His rendition was enthusiastic, but rather out of tune.

The postman continued along the isolated farm track, keeping a wary eye on his rear-view mirror, he needed to know who was behind him. He felt tense, vulnerable – the white van was still there. They'd followed him closely for nearly ten miles. Something didn't feel right. Was he being silly, over-reacting perhaps? Surely, they were only a couple of workmen – no need to panic. He nodded. I bet they're going to repair Len McCormack's leaking roof, yes, that'll be it. That farmhouse is in a terrible state! Len said he'd found someone who was prepared to fix the roof, but they were struggling to find the right type of Welsh slate, it had to match the old stuff.

The postman tried not to think about Dave Prentis, one of his workmates. Poor old Dave had been beaten-up the previous month and every one of his parcels stolen. Dave had been alone too, driving down a deserted county lane, seven miles to the west of Basingstoke…

Once the farmer's mail had been pushed through his letterbox (car tax reminder and a few items of junk mail) the postman made a three-point turn and set off for home. He was looking forward to beef stew and dumplings, made by Joyce, his beloved wife of thirty-three years…

After half a mile, it was necessary to brake sharply, put the gear-stick in neutral and apply the handbrake. The muddy track was blocked by the white van, it must have broken down. Two suspicious-looking characters were standing beside it, neither man acknowledged him…

Oh well, perhaps he could be of assistance, he certainly knew a thing or two about car engines. He smiled and nodded as he walked nervously towards them. For his kindness, he received several violent punches to his kidneys – the pain was excruciating. He cried out, crumpled, then fell to the ground…

One man drove home in the Royal Mail van, his accomplice following closely in the filthy white van.

It was nearly an hour before farmer McCormack discovered the postman's body. Len rang for an ambulance but it didn't arrive for thirty-five minutes. Bob Higgins had died from a massive stroke. He was fifty-six, slim, a non-smoker and in excellent health. The previous month, Bob had completed his seventh London marathon in under five hours, beating his previous time by nineteen minutes.

The brothers hadn't intended to kill Bob Higgins, so they felt no guilt whatsoever. These things happen. They had to silence him – they needed his van. Paddy didn't know his own strength, no more than that…

It was a beautiful morning in early May; not a cloud in the sky. The O'Reilly brothers were up bright and early. Joseph looked at his brother. "Now then Paddy, we have to clone a number plate, so, we'll go for a drive. We must choose a Royal Mail van that's the same make and year as ours. There's bound to be a few, out and about, doing their deliveries."

Patrick was grinning like a Cheshire cat; a rather clever idea had popped into his head. He'd be the first to admit, it wasn't something that happened very often. He looked at his watch, ten past five. "Why don't we drive to the depot, in Brighton? At this time of day, there'll be dozens of vans parked in the yard. They don't all go out at the crack of dawn. We can take our pick."

Joseph was impressed. Patrick struggled to read and write, but on occasions, yes, he'd have a cracking idea!

"Who's a clever boy then?" Joseph slapped his brother on the back. "That's brilliant. Well done. I'd better write down what we're looking for: it's a Ford Fiesta van, a *Courier Kombi*.

"Ah, that's a stupid name, so it is! The post office started using them in 2012, so we'll soon find one the same year as *our* red van."

The brothers considered the stolen Royal Mail van to be their property. It was on their land, therefore, it belonged to them. *'Finders, keepers, losers, weepers,'* that was the name of the game.

"We'll have a nip or two of whiskey before we set off, steady the nerves, even though we've had no breakfast!" Joseph laughed. "I suppose I'd better drive, Paddy, you get over-confident when you've been drinking. This is an important day, we don't wanna get stopped for speeding, do we? It would spoil our plans."

Just after lunch, brand-new number plates had been attached to the small red van. Paddy gave them an unnecessary spit-and-polish...

Joseph had enjoyed flirting with the sales assistant in Halfords; she was a skinny woman, plain, but with beautiful, curly blonde hair. She'd piled her hair on top of her head, leaving loose a number of curly whisps which Joseph found quite sexy. He stood as close to her as he dared. Luckily for her, it was only two days since his last shower.

Joseph smiled, displaying a row of neat white teeth. He ran his fingers slowly through his hair in an attempt to show how thick, clean and shiny it looked. Once again, his good looks could be relied upon to help him get what he wanted.

Patrick strolled around the store putting small objects into his jacket pocket. The CCTV cameras were at the far end of the building, by the exit, so he kept out of their way. Besides, he always stood next to a customer, using them as a shield as the stolen items were squirreled away.

The name Melanie was pinned on the assistant's uniform. "Now then Melanie, I'd like some new number plates, if you'd be so kind. Guess what? Our late mother, God rest her soul, was called Melanie. Just like you, she was a real beauty."

For the first time in many years, Melanie blushed. Good looking men didn't flirt with ordinary women like her! These two guys were as rough as hell, probably Irish gypsies, but they were very handsome. She loved their big brown eyes and long lashes. They possessed an animal magnetism that she couldn't explain or resist…

Melanie looked worried. "Oh, dear, I'm not sure what to do. I'm afraid you'll have to provide me with all the paperwork before I can issue replacement number plates. It's the law, you know, rules and regs. I assume you *are* the registered owners?"

"Oh, bless your heart, me darlin', sure we are, we've had the van since new, it's our pride and joy. I'm sorry, I left all the paperwork on the kitchen table. I'll tell you what's been happening; it's our nephew, Bernie, he's learning to drive, he keeps reversing into things, he's such a rascal. Yesterday, he clipped our beautiful rockery and dented the rear number plate, so I said to Seamus, he's me brother – that's him over there, looking at cans of WD40 – we'd best get some new plates made up. Bernie's a little devil, he's got scrapes on the front number plate too! So, in a nut shell, that's why we're here."

He winked. Melanie blushed again; she was beginning to feel flustered.

"Oh, alright then. Perhaps it doesn't matter, as long as no-one tells the boss. Promise me you won't tell anyone? *Not ever?* I enjoy working here, I don't want to get the sack."

Joseph gave her hand the lightest of touches. "I could never do such a thing – not to a lady like you. Tomorrow, you'll be getting some roses – I'll send 'em here. It'll make all the other ladies jealous, so make sure no-one else gets their sticky hands on them."

Melanie giggled. Twenty minutes later, the number plates appeared...

Back home, with a cup of tea, they saw a funny side to the day's events.

Joseph shook his head and laughed. "From today there'll be *two* red vans driving around with identical number plates – we'd better not have an accident. Otherwise, we'll get some poor postie, who lives in Brighton, into a great deal of trouble!

First thing tomorrow I'll be sending a dozen red roses to that Melanie, she's a good girl. I'll tell you something, Paddy, we could do with a woman around the house. Since mammy died the place looks a mess and it smells a bit – although some of that's down to *Killer*: I wonder, should we give him a bath? When did we last change the sheets and duvet covers? Must be all of six months. Oh, yes, I remember now – the moment I pegged out the sheets and pillow cases it poured with rain. They stayed on the washing line for weeks, at one point they were frozen stiff, like the sails of a boat…"

Paddy chuckled then looked serious. "Do you think our Melanie can cook? You know, proper stuff – roast beef and Yorkshire pudding, dumplings, apple pies and cheese scones. Yes, that sort of thing. I'm telling you now, Joe, if she's gonna give us salads, day after day – no, sorry, she's not moving in."

Joseph nodded. "No need to worry, of course she can cook. Those plain women have to be good at domestic chores otherwise they'll never get themselves a decent man. She fancies me, alright, I could see the lust in her eyes. Shall I ask her to marry me? She'd love that. If she came and lived here, we'd be treated like kings, waited on hand and foot."

Paddy shook his head. "Just one problem, brother…

"These walls are quite thin, I'd have to hear all that malarky, night after night – you know what I mean – when you two were having sex. You can marry her on one condition; you must move down the landing to mammy's old room. It's nice and clean, she was only here for two years before she died."

Paddy made the sign of the cross on his chest.

Joseph chucked. "I've no problem with that, I can sleep anywhere. We've still got mammy's old feather mattress, I bet it could tell a tale or two. Our daddy was a real man: no wonder mammy always looked so tired! *Saints preserve us!* I'll have to move that painting of Jesus – it's hanging over mammy's bed, it'd put me right off. I'd best put it in the hall.

"Maybe I'll drive over to Halfords, tomorrow, deliver the roses, meself, see what Melanie says. I think she'll jump at the chance. I'm a fine-looking man."

Paddy nodded. Any woman in her right mind would be honoured and grateful to receive a proposal of marriage from someone as handsome as Joseph…

Chapter 15

Evil intentions...

The small red van (parked opposite the Gilby residence) had been there for over half an hour. Two middle-aged men sat inside, one gazing out of the driver's window, the other, head down, reading a tabloid newspaper.

The heavy oak gates started to open, electronically, but slowly. Now they were able to see the whole of Rupert's front garden, right up to the decorative porch, then, on its left, the double garage and sideway.

The driver smirked, nodded, then nudged his companion – a gritty expression on his face. *"This is it – the big one!"*

The men looked at each other, one suppressing a laugh, even though there was nothing remotely funny about their evil intentions. Neither man appeared to possess a conscience, for them, this day was long-overdue. After months of debate and heated arguments, their despicable, spine-chilling plans were about to become a reality…

Anyone walking casually past the red van (who had their wits about them) would sense immediately, something wasn't right. The van belonged to the Royal Mail, so, who were these scruffy individuals? Yes, *two* men – clearly a driver and a passenger. Why were they smoking cigarettes without opening a single window, thus filling their van with toxic, greyish-blue smoke? They looked anxious: both men slouched in their seats, hoping to look like genuine workmen. For what reason were they parked in an up-market residential area? Perhaps they were waiting for someone. However, the most perplexing question of all would have to be – why was neither man wearing a postman's distinctive uniform?

Members of the pubic see things, worrying things, but how many actually telephone 999?

The men watched, enthralled, as Roxy climbed into her brand-new BMW convertible. They looked spell-bound. Perhaps this was the first time they'd encountered a woman like Roxy, in the flesh… So beautiful, so elegant, so refined.

"Bloody hell," whispered one to the other, "never mind the flippin' car – will you take a look at those legs? That young woman looks even lovelier than she does on the cover of those glossy magazines!"

Rupert stared out of the study window, watching his wife's departure, his expression anything but happy. Roxy smiled sweetly, then waved in his direction. She revved the engine for several minutes, the sole purpose being to infuriate her spouse. The car was driven away at high speed, spraying pea gravel in all directions.

Rupert shook his fist, "You stupid bitch, you'll ruin the paintwork!"

Her marriage to Rupert, splashed across a variety of newspapers, had given her a great deal of free publicity which led, indirectly, to further modelling contracts.

Roxy's name was the latest addition to an imaginary, but nevertheless, fascinating and lengthy list. The list is no more than a collection of names; celebrities, authors, artists, singers, sporting heroes and even talentless wannabees.

They have but one thing in common: they can be identified, immediately, by a single name.

The name '*Roxy*' would be joining (amongst many others) *Banksy, Monet, Picasso, Dickens, Shakespeare, Chaucer, Einstein, Freud, Elvis, Kylie, Madonna, Beyonce, Twiggy, Hitler, Kennedy, Churchill, Tiger, Pele, Navratilova and Ronaldo.*

The Gilby's recently acquired home had been named *The Cherry Orchard* by the previous owner, retired army officer, Colonel Reginald Phelps. For anyone of notoriety or perhaps just wishing to splash the cash, Little Common, on the outskirts of Bexhill, was a desirable place to live. The 'common land' (as it had been known for centuries) was tree-lined and always well-maintained. With plenty of room for people to walk their dogs and for children to play in a safe environment, houses and bungalows were snapped up the moment they appeared on the market. The previous month, a shabby, two-bedroomed semi, with large rear garden, had been sold for over half a million pounds, which pleased the residents, it kept out the undesirables…

The men crept slowly along the Gilby's sideway, heads down, relieved to see they were hidden from sight by a neighbour's large wooden shed and tall brick wall. Would the back-door be unlocked?

One of them pointed to the far end of the garden; in amongst mature trees and evergreen shrubs, a man wearing a grey T shirt and faded jeans was busy filling up the bird-feeders. A plastic bucket containing sunflower hearts was by his side. Yes, it was him alright, they'd know him anywhere.

A Taser, on loan from an Albanian drug dealer, was fired at Rupert, he fell to the ground, unable to move. The men looked at each other, open mouthed. They'd never used such a weapon before; however, they needn't have worried, it was fantastic! Kreshnik had promised them they wouldn't be disappointed. They'd given him £500 – he'd laughed and said, *'I am generous man, you, keep it for month.'* They'd nodded and patted him on the back: a couple of days would be more than enough…

Storm clouds were gathering; no doubt a heavy downpour would follow. The light was fading too, they must be on their way. If it rained, they would leave footprints on the edge of the lawn, that would never do. Many criminals had been caught, even sent to prison – simply because of the unusual or easily identified pattern on the sole of their trainers…

A wheelbarrow had been left next to the shed – perfect. Just the thing for transporting a body down towards the house.

Rupert's hands were secured with cable ties and a gag stuffed inside his mouth. A cotton pillow case was pulled over his head. One of the men hurried across the road and climbed into the red van. He parked it in front of the sideway, thus enabling them to pull and drag Rupert into the back.

Luckily for them, Rupert *had* left the back door unlocked, giving them access to the whole house.

Very little cash had been found, which was hardly surprising, but still disappointing. Debit and credit cards had certainly taken the fun out of burglary! Gone were the days when sideboard drawers contained purses and wallets full of cash. Paper money was hidden under feather mattresses or inside an old teapot, vase or biscuit tin.

Nevertheless, a rummage through Roxy's jewellery box was most rewarding: three antique rings (they assumed the diamonds, rubies and sapphires were genuine) plus gold chains and a gentleman's watch. The watch was a *Rolex Oyster Perpetual with black dial,* incredibly rare, incredibly expensive. After being wrapped in a grubby handkerchief, it went straight inside the man's jacket pocket, he had no idea of its value. It meant nothing to him – no more than if it were a *Timex.*

A small drawer in Roxy's dressing table was pulled open; an item of underwear was removed. The man laughed salaciously, putting the black lace panties on his head.

The other man nodded, breathing heavily. "Oh, yes, *black lace panties,* my favourite – get a pair for me! You know how I love a trophy."

Much as they would have enjoyed staying longer in the couple's bedroom, examining Roxy's underwear, they decided to leave, after all, they had no idea when she might return…

Halfway home, Rupert tried calling for help, but with a gag in his mouth, all he could manage were muffled sounds. The men threw back their heads and laughed – this was great fun and an easy way to get rich…

The van stopped. For a few moments, silence. With a man either side of him, Rupert was guided towards a derelict barn. His hands were released from the cable ties and the gag removed from his mouth; the pillow case was once again pulled over his head.

"If you behave yourself, matey, we might bring you a bottle of water and something to eat – if not, you can starve to death. It's your choice, Sunny Jim…"

Rupert was terrified. What on earth was going on? Where was he? He wondered how long he'd been paralysed; it must have been longer than thirty minutes. He could remember waking up in the back of the van, he'd tried to call out.

The man's voice sounded odd, as if he were trying to disguise his accent. He sounded like a Londoner, maybe a Cockney, but occasionally he forgot and lapsed into his native tongue – the result was a mish-mash of accents. He could have been born in Wales, Scotland or Ireland. If Rupert had been at the cinema, he would have found these amateurs very amusing…

Of one thing he was sure, he'd been kidnapped. It would be his father, not Roxy, who'd be asked to pay the ransom. How much was he worth? £50,000? £100,000? He smiled weakly; maybe, like the Mona Lisa, he was priceless. Suddenly, a lack of water and stark terror overwhelmed him – he lost consciousness.

Someone was shaking him quite violently. The pillow case was removed and thrown to the ground. One of the men placed a plastic tray on a bale of straw; a mug of sweet tea, two chocolate digestives and a cheese sandwich; more than he'd been expecting.

"Keep quiet, Rupert, be a good boy, no shouting, then you won't get murdered." The man laughed.

He must remember that tattoo – yes, a snake, winding around the man's forearm. The men were wearing balaclavas and aviator-style sunglasses – nevertheless, there was definitely something familiar about them...

Chapter 16

Where is Rupert?

Driving through the Sussex Downs had been exhilarating. Whilst on the back roads, Roxy put her foot down, reaching speeds of over 90 mph, her hair streaming out behind her, but only when, in her opinion, it was safe to do so.

Winston, her little pug, sat in the back seat; as long as he was with his mistress, he didn't care where they went, or what speeds they achieved. Roxy would never exceed the speed limit in a village or built-up area, she wasn't selfish, she wasn't reckless. She was a lady who loved life and anything that gave her a thrill, the reason why she'd been attracted to Rupert.

Roxy's head was awash with thoughts; she must get everything in order…

We'll be coming and going all weekend so I shall leave Winston with Hugo and Alicia – they love having him, it gives them an excuse to go for a long walk. As it's Thursday, I may as well drop him off now. She smiled; they can see my new car too!

Roxy's life had changed for the better; she'd fallen madly in love with Danny Dawson, even though no-one would call him thrilling or exciting. Danny had many good qualities: he was honest, supportive, faithful, warm and loving. In her eyes, perfect…

When Roxy arrived home, she couldn't find her husband. How odd, she thought, he didn't say he was going out. A mug of coffee, hardly touched, was on the kitchen table; it was stone cold.

With torch in hand, she went outside to see if he was in the garden – it was almost dark – no sign of him. Two bird feeders were lying on the grass, they were full, so she hung them up in one of the cherry trees. The bucket, containing sunflower seeds, had been left outside, something Rupert would never do. It was kept in the garden shed – he didn't want to encourage vermin.

Although Rupert and Roxy spent very little quality time together, if one of them should go out unexpectedly, they'd text or leave a note on the kitchen table. She smiled; no doubt he's nipped out for cigarettes – in that case he won't be long. I do wish he'd give it up – it's a filthy habit…

The evening dragged; she missed Winston. Roxy sent several texts to her husband, the first one, just three words: 'Where are you?' but as yet, no reply. She knew, even before the ten o'clock news had finished, he wouldn't be home until the following day.

No doubt he was in a bad mood; he'd shouted at her once before when she sped off down the driveway sending gravel in all directions! She laughed, oh, dear, he'll have a right old go at me! Roxy continued to mull things over. Rupert must have gone to London on a whim – I suppose he got a taxi to the station. Yeah, he'll be dining out with *her,* his latest lover; they'll be spending the night at our apartment, *in our bed!* I bet he's carrying on with Desiree, that new girl from the Caribbean. Still, she is stunning and ten years younger than me…

Rupert had better remember our golden rule; before you leave, put the bottom sheet, pillow cases and duvet cover in the washing machine and don't forget to turn it on!

He'll be back tomorrow evening – it's not optional – it's my turn to stay in London this weekend. I shall treat Danny to fish and chips, we'll eat them in bed, it'll be fun!

Roxy giggled. "I shall leave the wrapping paper, dirty plates and cutlery for Rupert to clear up the following weekend. He'll be so angry!"

Chapter 17

Bluebell Cottage

The O'Reilly brothers were in a good mood; they liked Sundays, for them, it was still a day of rest. No matter how warm it was, they dozed before a roaring fire, their feet upon the brass fender. Empty cans of strong lager littered the floor. The television was turned on, although neither man intended to watch a repeat showing of David Attenborough's *Frozen Planet.*

A jar of pickled eggs passed between them; Joseph belched, loudly. "Any of those sarnies left?"

Patrick was proud of his latest 'creation' – beetroot, Spam and brown sauce sandwiches. An uncut loaf was essential as the slices of bread needed to be thick enough to support a vast amount of filling. Deep red vinegar soaked into the bread and ran down Joseph's chin, he wiped it off with the back of his hand.

He yawned, scratched a flea-bite on his thigh and cursed the dog. After his nap, he'd stroll over to the barn, Rupert might enjoy a few leftover sandwiches. He looked thoughtful: do posh folk, like Members of Parliament, eat Spam and beetroot? He chuckled. Unlikely, I'll tell him we're out of caviar!

Both men had holes in their socks which, incidentally, hadn't been washed for several days. Their socks and underpants were changed once a week, after a hasty shower. Neither man enjoyed getting wet: they used to laugh about it. Why would anyone (in their right mind) want to go through the unnecessary rigmarole of showering and changing their socks and underwear *every single day?* If they behaved in this stupid way, the washing machine would be turned on every single week! The kitchen reeked of damp, decay and neglect, which had been, on occasions, to their advantage. These lingering smells discouraged uninvited visitors from sitting down and making themselves at home. This 'heady aroma' was due to three things:

1: The sink was piled high with greasy pots and pans and the drain blocked – more often than not – with solidified bacon fat. Sometimes, when the ashtrays were full, cigarette ends were stubbed out on the stainless-steel draining board then rammed down the plug-hole with the aid of a teaspoon handle. Mammy wouldn't have allowed such shocking behaviour, although she'd been happy enough, cooking and cleaning for her beloved but wayward sons.

2: Two pairs of damp, filthy, wellington boots (worn when feeding the chickens, pigs and ponies) were placed on a folded newspaper and positioned close to the kitchen radiator. When the boots began to steam, the smell was intense. Visitors coughed, spluttered and put a protective hand over their nose and mouth.

3: The cheap dog food left out for *Killer,* had little nutritional value, but it managed to achieve an aroma similar to a runny, over-ripe French cheese.

The dog's bowl was refilled, but never washed or changed for another. Why bother when it was licked clean?

The previous tenants of Bluebell cottage were Bert and Olive Renton. Most evenings the family gathered together around the coal fire, it gave out a great deal of heat and became the focal point of the room…

Every Saturday evening, at seven o'clock sharp, Bert smoked a pipeful of tobacco before reading adventure stories to his close-knit family. Olive and the children were mesmerized by Bert's reassuring voice as he recounted stories to stir the imagination!

As the couple approached their nineties, they were persuaded to move into sheltered accommodation. They had mixed emotions, but it was a wise move, their new home was just five miles from their youngest daughter. Once they'd settled in, the landlord put Bluebell cottage on the market. The cottage was in a sorry state, no decorating or modernization had been carried out for decades – it would be a tricky place to sell. A local builder had applied, more than once, for planning permission: *'Demolition of Bluebell cottage, with three detached houses and two bungalows built in its place.'*

The application was turned down, without further ado. Access to any new-build properties, plus the amount of infrastructure required would be detrimental to the nearby *Site of Special Scientific Interest (SSSI)*. The purple 'angel wing' orchid had been discovered in one of the Renton's set-aside fields and must be protected at all costs. During the previous ten years, only one other site in the south of England had produced photographic evidence of this rare orchid. For obvious reasons the exact location had to be kept under wraps. The O'Reilly brothers weren't remotely interested in rare orchids, although it had crossed Joseph's mind that a few orchids could be dug up and sold to wealthy buyers, via the internet…

Meanwhile, if Miss Nancy Musgrove, the lady from *Natural England,* intended to give them a generous sum of money (annually) to leave the field exactly as it was, so be it. They were happy to continue with the legal agreement signed by Bert and Olive Renton.

Miss Musgrove's visit was brief, she appeared nervous, jumpy and in a hurry to leave. The sofa was stained in several places: tea, coffee, strong lager and of course, beetroot. Nancy declined an invitation to sit down even though *Killer* had been pushed roughly off the sofa to make room for her. The dog gazed at her with fear in his eyes. Nancy stroked his back and whispered to him. He relaxed. This lady was nothing like his owners, she was kindly, she would never hurt him. Why couldn't he go home with her?

Miss Musgrove shook her head. No thanks, she didn't want a cup of tea or a jam doughnut. The brothers looked surprised: perhaps she was unfamiliar with such generosity.

The following month, several official looking papers were signed by the brothers, then witnessed by a solicitor; all costs met by *Natural England.*

That night, the God-fearing brothers recited an extra prayer, together, before they retired to bed. This windfall was like manna from heaven…

Miss Musgrove's department dealt with environmental issues, the reason why she was close to her cousin, Robert. He, however, had a more challenging clientele – those who thought it acceptable to dump waste material, even asbestos, in country lanes.

Robbie lived in Oxford, Nancy, on the outskirts of Reading. They emailed each other regularly, compared notes and discussed pressing issues. Nancy worked mainly from home, but her job involved travelling thousands of miles each year.

She could remember, quite vividly, Robbie telling her the story behind the dumping of asbestos sheeting and roofing tiles in Lower Foxton, a delightful Cotswold village. The village was known for its architecturally pleasing (but now derelict) windmill. Robbie had been livid at the time, but luckily, the culprits had been traced and given a heavy fine, although they'd avoided a prison sentence...

Rupert Gilby, former director of Gilby, Smythe and Boothroyd, had purchased the site. He'd received a huge fine and ordered to pay the clear-up fee. However, the magistrate insisted Gilby's behaviour had been naïve rather than anti-social. He thanked him for passing on information that enabled the police to trace the culprits who'd removed, then dumped, the carcinogenic asbestos. The magistrate had glared in Rupert's direction, then remarked:

"As a man from a well-respected family, and one of the country's most prominent merchant bankers, one would expect Mr Gilby to act responsibly and check the qualifications of those whom he chooses to employ!"

Nancy was impressed by cousin Robbie's tenacity. Vital and damning evidence had been provided by the contents of a flattened, Boots carrier bag: quite remarkable.

Robbie often had a fascinating tale to tell, however, they had a rule, the names of clients (especially the violent type) were best kept secret. Locations too were changed, if and when Robbie thought it was necessary.

Nancy much preferred her chosen career. Dealing with rare orchids and other protected species was safer and more fun than the scary world of asbestos, fly-tipping and violent criminals…

Chapter 18

Rupert tries to remain positive

Rupert was fast asleep, due to boredom rather than weariness, although his body ached through lack of exercise. He guessed, incorrectly, he'd been kept in the barn for over a month. If only he'd been able to mark the days by scratching notches on something with his plastic spoon or fork. The men had refused to given him a knife of any description.

Although balaclavas were still in use, the aviator sunglasses had been discarded. Both men were becoming careless; when speaking to Rupert, the phoney accents had been dropped altogether. They seemed blissfully unaware that an Irish accent was something difficult to disguise.

When the penny dropped and he realized the identity of his captors, Rupert felt a strange but understandable sense of relief – *better the devil you know…*

The O'Reilly brothers were dangerous: they were thieves, conmen and heartless bullies. Rupert tried to remain positive – he'd nothing to fear – they wouldn't hurt him, they just wanted easy money. Once they'd collected the ransom, they'd drive him somewhere remote and he'd have to make his own way home. He chuckled, thinking, I hope they don't leave me somewhere like the New Forest, in the middle of the night. I'd be terrified, I might get attacked by huge owls or bats! Even a New Forest pony would be scary in the dark. What if it was cold and pouring with rain? I might die from exposure!

He heard the barn door being unlocked, it brought him back to reality. His shoulder muscles tightened. Patrick stood before him; a solid man, weighing in at over sixteen stone.

"Here's two litres of coke; it'll keep you going. Will you look at what I've made for you? Tis a fine sandwich and no mistake. Me best creation yet: beetroot, grated cheese, mayo and Spam. Look – I've got yer two sheets of kitchen paper, I bet you've never seen it before! We're quite posh, really."

Rupert laughed. *"Wow! Michelin starred food and kitchen paper. You are spoiling me. I can imagine the headlines – kidnap victim kept in luxurious surroundings!"*

Patrick looked angry. He poked Rupert with a grubby finger. "You can stop that, right now! Enough of your sarcasm. You've been a good boy, quiet as a mouse, don't push your luck. Anyway, here's a couple of presents for you."

To his surprise, the previous day's Daily Telegraph was placed at the bottom of his flimsy camp-bed, then a packet of twenty cigarettes was thrown in his direction, he grabbed them eagerly. Ah, Marlborough gold, king size. He'd been without a cigarette for what seemed an eternity. Patrick lit Rupert's cigarette for him. He wasn't about to hand over a box of matches – Rupert might decide to burn down the barn in a crazy attempt to escape!

Rupert smiled at his captor. "Fancy you remembering I smoked Marlborough gold. Oh, yes, of course, your family – well, the lads, nicked a whole packet of fags off me."

After Patrick left, locking the barn door behind him, Rupert read the newspaper from cover to cover. He was disappointed, a few paragraphs, headed, *'More sightings of missing MP'* was all he could find. If things had been different and the article had been written about someone else, perhaps an opposition MP, he would have followed the story with glee.

Rupert frowned. What sort of person contacts a daily newspaper when a politician or celebrity goes missing? Someone desperate for attention – that's who. He read the article for a second time.

Apparently, the MP for Bexhill on sea and Pevensey Bay, Rupert Gilby, had been spotted on the Orient Express, en route to Paris!

"Oh, yeah?" he whispered. "Was the delectable Desiree sitting beside me on the train?"

A loyal member of the Green Party felt obliged to photograph Rupert in Waitrose, Rushden branch. He appeared to be chatting to a young Asian woman. The email had been sent by a man calling himself 'Trevor.' He'd attached the photograph to his email, with an apology. 'Sorry, the imagine is a bit blurry; I did my best but Mr Gilby was over the other side of the store, you know, by the frozen chips and peas. It's odd really, I was the only person watching him from behind the fruit and veg.'

The silliest sighting by far, was left until last: Rupert burst out laughing. Apparently, Mr Gilby was spotted driving a yellow Reliant Robin, recklessly, in the fast lane of the M25, just after junction eleven, the Chertsey interchange. There was certainly a likeness, similar features, but on closer examination the coloured photograph revealed the driver had ginger hair!

Rupert stared at the washing-up bowl half-filled with tepid water, the threadbare bath towel, the face cloth, and the brand-new bar of Dove soap. He tutted. I can imagine what life was like for the working classes during the Victorian era; no bathroom, no inside toilet and certainly no privacy.

He shivered. "It was chilly last night; I'll ask for another blanket. Oh, hell, I smell like a wet dog. I'd give anything for a shower…"

The brothers had become fond of Rupert, especially Patrick, who was treating him like a sheep dog who must be kept inside the barn until fully trained. Even the much-hated cotton pillow case had been taken away, never to be seen again. On occasions, *Killer* sneaked inside the barn looking for Rupert – he'd rather be with a stranger than his cruel owners. His bark was worse than his bite – Rupert had no fear of him. He'd gained another, far smaller companion, a brown mouse. If he threw down morsels of food, it ran back and forth, then scuttled back to its home. The mouse wasn't a fan of beetroot but tiny pieces of Spam, cheese or bread were soon whisked away.

The brothers understood why Rupert had 'grassed them up.' He'd been persuaded to do so in order to reduce the heavy fine he'd been facing. Anyone would have done the same.

The previous week, Hugo and Alicia had received a letter that shook their world; the kidnappers were demanding a ransom of £75,000. The brothers had enjoyed designing their 'mini masterpiece.' They were copying a scene from their favourite film, 'Pay Up or She Dies,' an obscure black and white movie from the 1950s. Words, letters and numbers were cut from the pages of the *Daily Mirror* and *Woman's Own* magazine then pasted onto a sheet of A4 paper:

We have Rupert IF you *WANT* to see him AGAIN leave **£75,000** in cash in **jiffy bag** next to **POST-BOX** outside Alexander House **Hastings.** *Thursday* 25th at 3.30pm. Don't **CONTACT** Police OR **Rupert** will be **MUR***DERED.*

Alexander House, headquarters of the East Sussex Building Society, was in Albert Road, a busy part of town. A block of flats had just been completed, squeezed in between a parade of shops and the newly renovated primary school.

D.S. Sophie Hollis was impressed; the kidnappers had given a lot of thought to their chosen time and place. At three-thirty, Albert

Road would be buzzing with parents or child-minders. Over three hundred excitable children needed to be picked up and taken home…

She looked across at her boss and frowned. "There'll be cars parked on double yellow lines and the pelican crossing will be in constant use. Spotting the kidnappers is going to be tricky.

"Still, their letter gave something away, didn't it? It said, *'we have Rupert,'* not *'I have Rupert.'* Interesting. Must be at least two of 'em."

Her boss shrugged but didn't say a word. Working alongside D.I. Peter Buxton was going to be a challenging experience. His reputation went before him – he didn't suffer fools gladly.

Sophie felt obliged to tell him she'd been to a party at Rupert Gilby's parent's home.

This time he managed a terse reply, although his patronizing attitude towards the young detective sergeant was unforgivable.

"So? You are telling me because?"

Sophie's cheeks turned pink. Pete was due to retire the following spring – he'd be fifty at the end of April. His lack of good manners towards a colleague gave the distinct impression he'd had more than enough!

Arriving early, Pete and Sophie managed to find a parking space opposite the post-box.

Sometimes, a bright colour can be more effective than something bland, the reason why he'd borrowed Mrs Buxton's twelve-year-old mini. No-one, going under cover, would choose a bright green car! Pete was an outsider: he made his own rules. He wouldn't be granted permission to use his wife's car for a covert operation – no, not in a million years.

At three-twenty, Hugo Gilby, looking pale and jittery, placed the jiffy bag next to the post-box. Aware of just how much money was inside, he felt unhappy leaving it unattended.

"Look, over there," whispered Sophie, pointing to a man wearing a postman's uniform, "he's walking towards the post-box."

Pete tutted, "Course he is – he's the flamin' postman! The post-box is emptied at three-forty, he's just turned up early, that's all."

Sophie felt agitated. *"Yes, I know that, but I think we ought to get out and…"*

Receiving another sideways glance from Buxton, she stopped, mid-sentence…

A morbidly obese, highly tattooed woman, wearing a black sleeveless-top and bright-pink shorts, pushed her way through a group of mums, then stood right in front of the post-box, blocking the detectives' view. She shouted at her daughter, glared at her small son, then dropped a few letters in the box.

Eventually, the tattooed woman and her kids moved away. They could see the postman now, running back to his van which had been parked on the opposite side of the road. He was carrying a brown sack; he must have emptied the post-box whilst hidden from view. He leapt into the passenger seat; the red van drove away at high speed and with a squeal of tyres. Heads turned, parents grabbed hold of their children and someone's granddad ran into the middle of road trying to make a note of the van's number plate. Unfortunately, he wasn't wearing his spectacles. KW62 was all he could decipher.

Even the van's hasty departure failed to raise D.I. Buxton's blood pressure, that is, until Sophie shouted, *"That must have been them – you idiot! The jiffy bag has gone!"*

They'd failed miserably and allowed the kidnappers to drive off with £75,000. Sophie was furious. "Oh my God, they must think it's their lucky day."

Pete's face looked pale and clammy. "We've blown it, haven't we? Yeah, and it's all my fault. I think the less said about this, the better. If you wanna stay in the CID, you'll stick to the story, okay? Right, *this* is what happened:

"The fat woman with the big arse, pink shorts and two kids was blocking our view. After she went into the sweet-shop, we could see the post box, but it was too late, the jiffy bag had disappeared."

Sophie was shocked, she shook her head, what the hell was wrong with him? They should have stepped out of his wife's car, watched the postman empty the letter-box (or not, as the case may be) then arrested him if he picked up the jiffy bag. Instead, they sat in the car, *doing absolutely nothing.* More to the point – should she tell a pack of lies in order to cover up her boss's ineptitude? No way.

Her boss was a nightmare, he'd made a mess of everything and he knew it. All they'd managed to do was sit quietly in Mrs Buxton's bright green car. They should have followed the red van discreetly and at a safe distance. Pete seemed in a permanent daze, unable to make decisions. It may have turned out to be a complete waste of time, but on the other hand, the van might have taken them straight to Rupert Gilby. If nothing else had been achieved, they could have arrested the postman for exceeding 30mph in a built-up area! Poor Rupert. It was over three weeks since his disappearance, was he still alive?

The kidnappers collected the money, but were they prepared to let him go? Unlikely…

Chapter 19

Patrick makes a foolish mistake

The brothers felt a degree of empathy towards their victim. A less confident man, having been locked up in a barn for a few weeks, might have become a nervous wreck; crying, shouting or begging to be set free! Rupert had no idea when or even if his captors would release him. His cheerfulness was commendable, although, when he greeted them with a smile, they felt something akin to guilt…

They came from different backgrounds: there was a chasm between them. Rupert's calm acceptance of his terrifying ordeal was an example of courage; the O'Reilly brothers preferred brutish thuggery.

Joseph poured a tin of Heinz tomato soup into a small enamel saucepan; something with plenty of flavour and in his opinion, a meal fit for a king. Rupert would appreciate something other than apples or sandwiches with bizarre fillings.

The hot-plate was set at number nine. The soup boiled, spitting out orange blobs like a volcanic eruption. One hit Joseph's hand, another, his cheek. He cursed. The previous week a greasy chipolata landed on the hob and burned to a crisp. Still piping hot, it was thrown onto the floor for the dog. Now, every time the hot-plate was used, blue acrid smoke filled the air…

Joseph sighed. He ought to clean the hob, but not today, he wasn't in the mood; besides, since mammy died, they'd run out of cleaning products.

Adding a few necessary items to their shopping list hadn't occurred to them. They preferred buying what they referred to as 'essential items' – lager, Irish whiskey, cigarettes, ice-cream, chocolate, girly magazines, jars of pickled eggs and naturally – pickled beetroot for Paddy's famous sandwiches. If and when they remembered, they'd pick up a large box of dry dog food, the cheapest available…

Joseph added two slices of stale bread to the tray, then hurried across the yard.

Killer, chained up outside the barn, whimpered, the smell of hot food made him feel hungry: would this be another day when they'd forget to feed him?

A slice of bread was squeezed flat, by Rupert, then pushed under the barn door. It was grabbed, in seconds, by a grateful dog. Joseph didn't comment, but he shook his head, thinking, Rupert, you are a big softie.

This was the first time Joseph had noticed the packet of Marlborough gold, king size…

Once their terrified prisoner had settled down and enjoyed a cup of Patrick's strong tea, his pockets were emptied. Joseph could recall exactly what they'd discovered. His favourite item was the antique silver, Art Deco cigarette lighter, with *RPG* (Rupert Peregrine Gilby) engraved inside a small cartouche. It'd been one of Rupert's numerous twenty-first birthday presents.

To prevent any lengthy arguments over who deserved to keep the lighter, it was placed on the O'Reilly's fireplace as a useful ornament. A black leather wallet, with fifty pounds in cash and a couple of debit and credit cards had also been removed, along with a bunch of house keys. However, Joseph was positive, there had been no cigarettes. *Patrick must have given them to Rupert.* Surely, even he couldn't be that dumb...

Patrick was sitting in the kitchen, feet up, eating a jam doughnut; Joseph glared at him.

"Paddy, you are an eejit. I said buy him some fags and a newspaper, so what do you do? You buy him Marlborough gold, king size, his favourite brand. Why not go the whole hog? Yes, tie a red ribbon round the packet and write a message saying, *'With love from Paddy and Joe!'*

"Do you have any brain cells in that head of yours? Remember when we cleared out the Bexhill site? One of the lads – Callum, I think, nicked Rupert's fags – he'll not forget that in a hurry! *Any other brand would have done!*

"Sometimes I wonder if you're a genuine O'Reilly – you're nothing like our father, God rest his soul. He was a master of cunning."

Joseph made the sign of the cross.

"Our dear mammy must have had a lover, yes, a man thick as a plank, and you're his useless offspring!"

Patrick stared at the floor, he felt like a naughty schoolboy. He'd been expecting his brother to shout at him, telling him he was an eejit. He frowned, perhaps Rupert would have guessed the identity of his kidnappers even without the fags – well, it was hardly rocket-science! When given the cigarettes, Rupert had smiled and said, *'I've had withdrawal symptoms, you know, I feel quite shaky at times. Fancy you remembering my favourite brand, Marlborough gold, king size. I really appreciate it – cheers!*

Paddy was angry with himself, only too aware of what he should have done after hearing Rupert's grateful reply…

I should've grabbed the flaming cigarettes, chucked them in the bin, not left them in the barn for Joseph to discover. Why didn't I buy some more fags? Any old brand would have done. Patrick was getting a headache; he didn't like complicated situations…

Did Rupert think they'd kidnapped him *just* for the cash? Might there be another reason? Were the brothers seeking to punish him because he'd given their names and details to the police?

Patrick's thoughts turned quickly to Elsie Lovage. Was Rupert aware they were the men in the mud-splattered van who'd tried to kidnap her? They wouldn't have hurt her, no, not a lady. She fought back like a she-wolf! She'd poked him in the eye, the bitch. If that damn bus hadn't turned up when it did, they'd have got her inside the van, somehow. His eye was red, sore and bruised for several days…

The other lot, the Dawsons, were good people. They weren't rich like the Gilby family but they'd have coughed up ten grand to get Mrs Lovage back, especially if they thought her life was in danger. Mrs Lovage's kidnapping had been intended as a trial run. They'd have kept *her* in the barn too. She'd have been a lot more trouble than Rupert! Patrick chuckled, "Oh yeah, quite a woman."

Joseph looked serious. "Listen up, will yer? Rupert has no idea where he is. He could be twenty, fifty or one hundred miles away from home. Don't forget, for much of the journey, he was unconscious. Still, it doesn't matter now, it's over – we'll have to kill him – we have no choice…

"If we let Rupert go, we'll be arrested within days. The cops know our address and have records of our fingerprints and DNA. There's no point having £75,000 hidden in the attic if we're in prison! I'll tell you something, dear brother, the maximum penalty for kidnapping is life, yes, life in prison. We'd hate being locked up, especially you with your claustrophobia…

"Oh, Paddy, if only you'd bought a different brand of cigarettes."

Joseph glared at his brother. "Tell me now, did you *always* wear yer balaclava? If

Gilby had any doubts about who we were, well, he hasn't now. Do you realise what you've done? You've all but signed Rupert's death warrant! *He'll not leave here alive…"*

Whenever Patrick was bullied or ridiculed by Joseph, he'd run upstairs and sit in mammy's room. He'd been very close to her: she'd protected him from the wrath of his brother.

Sometimes he'd cry, he still missed her, although he'd be mortified if anyone found out. O'Reilly men must be hard as nails, fearless and *never* shed tears.

Once, when staying with family members back in Ireland, Paddy managed to have a quiet word with the parish priest. 'Why am I such a weak man? I can't cope without her…'

Father Donovan replied, 'Don't take on so, my son, mammy is in heaven, with Jesus, they are watching over you. One day you'll be with her again and all your sins will be washed away. *Say three Hail Marys, you'll feel much better.'*

Chapter 20

The tale of Bridgette O'Reilly's pearls

Paddy rummaged through the top drawer of mammy's dressing table; it was full of fascinating things including her precious pearls. Next to the pearl necklace, in a small box, was a pair of matching earrings that could only be described as exquisite. Their value, at the time of his parents' wedding, was no less than fifteen hundred pounds. The earrings, with perfectly matched Japanese Akoya pearls, were made from 22 carat gold. This beautiful jewellery had been mammy's wedding present from Dermot, their late father, a man who'd been unemployed at the time of their marriage.

Whenever the family returned to Ireland, for weddings, baptisms or funerals, Dermot was persuaded to recount the fascinating story of *Bridgette O'Reilly's Pearls...*

Of course, back in the day, she'd been Bridgette Mary Murphy, the beautiful, carefree, seventeen-year-old sister of Dermot's best friend, Liam Cormac Murphy.

The O'Reilly family were devout Catholics: consequently, there were dozens of them. The hiring of a village hall was necessary for any serious celebrations.

It took no more than five pints of Guinness to get Dermot in the mood. Up he'd jump, full of enthusiasm and perform his piece like a true professional. Some of the story was invented or enhanced, but no-one cared; his family lapped it up! Dermot's amusing tale began just two weeks before the wedding...

He'd used nearly half a bottle of his sister's favourite, rose scented, bubble bath.

Much thought had been given to his appearance: he'd worn his best tweed suit, a brand-new white shirt and a Paisley-pattered cravat, a gift from Uncle Eammon. Carrying a silver-topped walking cane, he'd caught the early train to Dublin.

On entering *Abercorn and Blair,* a highly respected jeweller's shop (established in 1807) Dermot made a point of introducing himself as *Sebastian, the second son of Lord Kilkenny.* Surrounded by grovelling members of staff,

Dermot smiled, then, full of confidence, began his prepared speech…

'Now then, next month, my cousin, Martha-Louise, who lives in Belgravia with her sister, will be celebrating her twenty-first birthday. I intend to mark the day by buying her something rather special, a string of pearls with matching earrings. The price is of little interest, but they must be of the finest quality.'

The overtly camp shop assistant was in his element. Trays of earrings were removed from the shop's plate glass window and strings of pearls displayed artistically on dark blue velvet. The charming young customer was assured, on two occasions, Akoya pearls were the finest in the world…

Eventually, *Lord Kilkenny's second son* was satisfied, he'd chosen a string of pearls worth two thousand pounds.

This modest amount of money would have enabled Dermot to purchase a cottage in southern Ireland, complete with large garden and sea view. However, Dermot and Bridgette planned to enjoy married life in a brand-new caravan, keeping a biscuit tin full of cash beneath the bed. It was the only life they'd ever known.

Sebastian dithered and sighed over the earrings; which design should he choose? Large or small? Were large earrings considered vulgar? The moment the enthusiastic assistant rushed to the window for yet another tray, a pair of beautiful pearl earrings found its way into Dermot's jacket pocket.

When the assistant returned, Dermot frowned then ran his hands through his lovely, thick black hair. *"Oh dear, I'm more confused than ever. There are simply too many pairs to choose from!* Looking at jewellery is not a job for a man, so I'll tell you what I shall do. I'll buy the string of pearls, today, but I'll be back on Friday, with my mother, her ladyship, she'll know which earrings to buy."

He'd chuckled. "I'll tell you something, young man, my dear mama is an expert – she's inherited enough diamonds, rubies and emeralds to start her own jewellery shop!"

The assistant, Seamus O'Toole, was becoming obsessed with the handsome customer; he was magnificent – like a Greek statue. Seamus needed to sit down for a moment and catch his breath, he was feeling light-headed.

Sebastian was *so* attractive and his thick, dark hair was simply divine. He was wearing a distinctive after shave, although, not one Seamus recognised. Rather feminine too, like a bouquet of fresh roses. Unusual – for such a butch man.

Cheeky boy, was he flirting? How old was he? Surely no more than twenty-five. Interesting. He'd never had a liaison with an aristocrat…

No, stop it, Seamus, pull yourself together, that's just wishful thinking. He's a married man, he must be. He chuckled, yes, but who cares, so are many of my homosexual friends...

By now, Dermot O'Reilly was in need of another pint of Guinness: he was having the time of his life…

Dermot had always been a talented mimic, the life and soul of any party. His accent, when taking on the role of *Sebastian,* was flawless. Even when behaving in an effeminate way, his body language and vocabulary were spot on.

His story hadn't finished yet – that was just the first chapter. "You'll all be wondering, but too polite to ask, where did Dermot get two thousand pounds from? Ah, listen, cos I'll be telling yer.

"The previous month, me and me brother Sam, broke into a post office. We selected a pretty little village called Derrybridge – oh, yes, miles away from home it was. We cut the wires to the alarm and in we went! A mean thing to do, I'll grant you, but these folks are always insured. It was a Thursday night, the safe was full to bursting with pension money and child benefit, all ready for the following day, so we helped ourselves. Over four and a half thousand pounds we got. A good night's work and no mistake!

"Now then, me darlin' family – the drinks are on me!"

Dermot expected and received a standing ovation for his colourful tale…

Chapter 21

Death comes to us all

Patrick smiled; yes, their father had been a one-off. The string of pearls was returned to its velvet lined box, then placed in the drawer beside a smaller box containing the exquisite Akoya pearl earrings.

Paddy examined the small tinted bottle containing his mother's prescription medicine – it hadn't been touched since the day she died. He sighed, poor mammy, she'd been in a lot of pain. Still, she'd be happy now, in heaven, with those who'd gone before…

Joseph read the Daily Mirror from cover to cover, he liked to get his money's worth. Sadly, even with coaching from his brother, Patrick's reading age failed to rise above ten. On a good day, he could read short words without stumbling: tarmac, beer, whiskey, dog, pretty, lady and money. Yes, these were nice words, they made sense, he wasn't scared of them. Nevertheless, he would never attempt to read a label from the pharmacy for fear of making a fool of himself. Sometimes he felt intimidated by these horrible long words, they looked 'jazzy' as if moving around on the page, trying to confuse him and make him look silly.

He handed the small bottle to Joseph, who grabbed it and glared at his brother. "Why on earth would you be showing me mammy's pills, for God's sake?"

"Well, Joe, they're very strong, aren't they? Oh, goodness me – I've just remembered the name, I can say it, but I can't read it, the letters look fuzzy. It's Oxycodone! Daisy, the nurse who looked after mammy said we must *never* take them; they are nothing like paracetamol. They are only for people in a lot of pain, to help them sleep.

"I thought we could crush three or four and put them in Rupert's drink, you know, knock him out with drugs before we kill him. To be honest, it'll be easier than I thought – these are capsules, we can snip off the top and pour the Oxycodone straight into his drink – well, how about that?"

Joseph was impressed by his brother's ingenuity. He lit a cigarette, nodded and handed it over. "Here we are, brother, have a drag."

Paddy, so often careless and confused, had done it again! It'd been Paddy's inspirational idea to visit the Royal Mail depot in Brighton, find an identical van, then clone the number plate. So much quicker and easier than driving around for days until they found one!

Once Rupert was in a deep, drug-induced sleep, a plastic bag would be pulled over his head and secured with thick garden twine, but *not before* cable ties had been attached to his wrists. A clean and tidy kill – no blood or guts…

What better place to bury a body than a *Site of Special Scientific Interest?* Most of the purple 'angel wing' orchids were growing in the shade, underneath the hawthorn hedge, planted way back in the 1920s.

Rupert's body would be buried in the centre of the field, beside an ancient oak tree where, fingers crossed, it would never be found. As ideas went, it was brilliant; such irony! They would continue to receive thousands of pounds each year from *Natural England* as long as they left the field exactly as nature intended. Well, no problem there, apart from the unusual and macabre addition of a man's body.

"I'll tell you something, Paddy me boy, after that stroke of genius, I shall be buying you a posh car: one to impress the ladies...

"We have £75,000 to spend. We'll get you a second-hand Jag, you've always wanted one. Silver, or black if you prefer. We mustn't be too flashy and draw attention to ourselves, no, we'll buy one about three years old. With a car like that, you'll soon be getting yourself a woman...

"I suppose, one day, you ought to take a driving test, although I've never bothered – can't see the point and I've been driving since I was a youngster.

"It's the same with car insurance, crazy idea – why throw yer money away? Mind you, things are different now with computers and CCTV spying on us. I was telling Callum, he'd better take a driving test, odd though it might seem – it's not the sort of thing we do. He'll be passing first time, so he will, he's been driving on the road since he was thirteen. *Country lanes of course – well, okay, maybe on the motorway!"*

Paddy burst out laughing. If truth be told, since moving to England (to be closer to a few family members) they'd had some great times. Their father would've been very proud of them.

"Hey, Joe, do you remember when Callum drove us to Blackpool? It was his fifteenth birthday, he wanted to see the lights. Being such a tall lad, from a distance, he looked old enough to drive. Fantastic day, eight of us in that van: hot dogs, candy floss, pretty girls and donkey rides. Callum was the only one who remained sober!

"All was fine and dandy until Callum backed into that red Ferrari, in the car park, right outside McDonalds. Yes, I remember now, it was the Welcome Break Services, Charnock Richard, on the M6. I have a good memory. I wonder what the owner said when he spotted the damage?"

After a nip or two of whiskey, the pair strolled over to the barn, they felt excited, not nervous or guilt-ridden. This was the first time they'd planned to murder anyone, but with careful planning, they'd be fine.

Sometimes they wished they'd never set eyes on Rupert Gilby, or spoken to him as he walked aimlessly round that derelict market garden in Bexhill-on-sea.

Rupert was reading a three-day-old Daily Telegraph. He was miffed – not a mention of his disappearance. Were the police still searching for him? By now, Roxy and his parents must be in melt-down. He sighed, longing for a cigarette, would they be bringing him another packet? He looked up, Paddy was smiling at him.

"Ah, Rupert, me boy, I bring you good tidings. Yer father coughed up all the money we asked for; you can be on your way. If you promise to keep your trap shut, you'll hear no more from us. *However, if you start blabbing to the police, we'll find you and kill you! Understand?"*

Rupert would have agreed to anything, even signed anything, as long as they set him free. He smiled to himself – he'd been no trouble. He'd decided, from day one, if he managed to stay positive, things would turn out alright in the end. He'd dozed during the day, but the nights had seemed endless and cold. He'd shed tears, feeling lonely and abandoned. That extra blanket he'd asked for had never arrived…

When feeling positive, he'd read every article in the Daily Telegraph, pushed food under the door for *Killer* and been entertained by a brown mouse.

Joseph made the first move. "Now then, before we drop you off, let's say, in Eastbourne, right by the railway station, let's have a drink together, show there's no ill feeling. Look, I've brought over a drop of the hard stuff – I've even poured it into a posh glass for you. Me and Paddy will have our drinks in one of yer paper cups."

Paddy had given Rupert an old stripy deckchair, he'd become quite fond of it; he sat back, raised his glass and said, "Cheers, lads, after today, I hope I shall never see your ugly mugs again!"

They laughed together, like old friends.

Rupert squinted and shook his head – it felt full of cotton wool; Paddy's voice sounded far away – then the barn began to spin. He gripped the sides of the deckchair, feeling terrified. Something wasn't right. He'd always been able to hold his drink, never had a problem before. Irish whiskey must be powerful stuff. Moments later, he slumped forward, his head upon his chest, he'd fallen into a deep sleep...

The brothers looked at each other, Joseph nodded – it was time to act. Pulling a plastic bag over the head of a man who is virtually unconscious, especially if his wrists are tied together, isn't too tricky, as long as you manage to avoid getting kicked by the frantic movements of his legs.

Once they'd achieved their aim, they turned their backs on Rupert, they couldn't bear to see his face, it was contorted, ugly and a deep shade of red. They heard a thump as his body fell, lifeless, to the floor.

Paddy looked pale, "I can't be doing with this, he looks awful, it's the stuff of nightmares…

"Come on, Joseph, let's go back indoors, it's time for *Deal or No Deal*. I like that Noel Edmunds. I'll make us some cheese on toast and a nice cuppa. No Spam, I promise!"

Chapter 22

A host of possible suspects

The very thought of interviewing Danny Dawson made D.S. Hollis feel uncomfortable. They'd been close, very close…

After the Gilby's eventful party, Danny made a wise decision; nothing would be gained and much lost by mentioning Sophie's emotional text, it would have caused a row between him and his parents. They were from a different generation they simply wouldn't understand. His parents had no idea Sophie had been watching when he'd held Roxy in his arms and kissed her longingly. Sophie had been shocked and extremely upset.

To save any unpleasantness, Danny told his parents he was very fond of Sophie, she was a great girl, but he didn't love her and he never would. They were disappointed, they would miss seeing her, but such is life. Their son would soon find another suitable girl.

One day, Danny would have to tell them about Roxy and how they'd fallen madly in love: he was dreading it. He'd have to convince them, this wasn't just a bit of fun, some short-lived infatuation, this relationship was forever. No doubt he'd receive a frosty and possibly sarcastic, response...

The Dawsons were asked to be discreet, the following information was for their ears only: *Rupert may have been kidnapped.* If so, time was of the essence, they must find him as soon as possible, his life could be in danger.

Fred and Jenny sat beside Danny. Their son might be a grown man, he'd just turned forty-one, but being interviewed as a possible 'person of interest' was not something to be taken lightly. Kidnapping carried a life sentence.

The questions asked were predictable: When did he last see Rupert? Had they fallen out over something? After Rupert and his boss bought the old market garden site, thus depriving Fred Dawson of his long-held dream, did their once close friendship become toxic?

What about Gilby's private life – any clues there? Might he be hiding-out somewhere? Any problems within the marriage, or financial worries? Would you be surprised to hear that Rupert was probably having an affair with his secretary, Desiree Marlow?

Danny looked angry. *"Blimey, give us a break, Sophie, you're asking an awful lot of questions...*

"Look, since Rupert became a member of parliament, I've hardly seen him. Politicians are not loved by the public, someone, a constituent for example, might have a grudge against him. There are some scary people out there. You need to speak to David Fanshawe, his boss, not me. He'll know Rupert's financial situation *and* if he's been involved with any dodgy business deals."

Danny narrowed his eyes before saying, "Why are you asking me about Rupert and Roxy's private life? Why would I know anything about it?"

Was Danny daring Sophie to say something she might regret, something designed to embarrass him?

After a cup of tea, Sophie left. She'd been convinced, even before interviewing Danny, he'd offer her nothing helpful or worth following-up on the subject of Rupert's disappearance. She'd hoped never to see him again but when her boss said, go and take a statement, it would have been unwise to argue.

D.I. Buxton was a nightmare, but now, at last, Sophie knew why. Getting the boss to open-up and trust her with his innermost feelings, had been like pulling teeth! He was an intensely private person who hated sharing his emotions; Sophie wondered if he came from a very 'uptight' family.

His wife of twenty-two years, Angela, had decided to move out, she could take no more of his miserable face, bad temper, excessive drinking and demanding job! She was moving to Newcastle, to live with her older sister, a widow. As a highly qualified nurse, Angela had much to offer, a job had been secured at the Royal Victoria Infirmary.

Buxton's team agreed, Rupert must have been taken against his will – presumably from his home in Little Common. Perhaps the kidnappers parked nearby and waited patiently until they saw Roxy drive away in her brand-new BMW. Despite numerous enquiries and members of staff trawling through hours of CCTV – they found no footage of him after his wife left the house. However, he had been picked up by one camera, at two-thirty that afternoon, chatting to an elderly lady in B&Q's car park, she'd dropped a silk scarf, Rupert picked it up and hurried after her. Sadly, this crisp and clear image would be of no use to anyone. Rupert's wife suggested checking the footage from the Esso garage, about three miles away, her husband shopped there, regularly, for cigarettes. Unfortunately, on the day in question, there'd been a problem with the camera so no footage was available…

Buxton and Hollis took the early train to London. Might this be the day when some of their probing questions received useful answers? Pete shook his head, if only they had something tangible to work on.

They had an eleven o'clock appointment with Gilby's closest friend, fellow Member of

Parliament, William Pilkington, son of the Minister without Portfolio, seventy-two-year-old Cedric Pilkington. William looked amazed when asked if Rupert had made enemies, especially amongst his constituents.

"Good Lord no, *don't be so ridiculous.* Rupert's such a charmer, everyone adores him. Never heard a bad word said against him."

Despite talking to several other members of parliament, including one lady from the Labour party and two gentlemen from the Liberal Democrats, no suggestions were forthcoming. Both detectives felt they were going nowhere fast.

During the train journey home, Sophie looked at her boss and frowned, saying, "No leads in Bexhill, Eastbourne or the House of Commons. Danny Dawson appears to be squeaky clean, so, where do we go from here?"

The drinks and snacks trolley rumbled through; they grabbed a cup of weak tea.

"There is *one* thing we should take a look at, Guv – what about Gilby's visit to Paris, with Desiree Marlow? I've been looking into her private life – she shares a flat in London with her cousin, Rosina, a legal secretary. I think it's in Pimlico. It would seem these two ladies are going places, working hard and studying too. Desiree's brother has been arrested a couple of times for receiving stolen property but that's all, nothing violent. Perhaps he's taken against Rupert, resents him having an affair with his sister. Although, kidnapping? Surely not! That's in a different league. It would be very difficult to keep someone locked-up in the East End of London!

"Do you remember Jeremy Rainsford, the M.P. for Wokingham? The chap we spoke to on the way out – wearing a purple tie? Well, he was convinced there was something going on between Rupert and Desiree. He'd seen them in a restaurant, just the two of them, very cosy. *'You could tell by the way they looked at each other,'* he said, then winked. Roxy knows Desiree accompanied Rupert to Paris the other week. Oh yes, she'd noticed an unfamiliar perfume on his new white shirt. By the way, Guv, the trip was work, not pleasure. Humm, shall we say, a bit of both?"

Pete Buxton looked across at Sophie, raised an eyebrow, then burst out laughing. *"Yes, Sophie, of course it was – and if you believe that, you'll believe anything!"*

Sophie sighed, wow, what a relief, he *was* human after all. She'd made him laugh, which in her opinion was quite an achievement. She removed a small plastic box from her tote bag.

"Here you are, Sir, have a piece of my mum's ginger cake, it's lovely and moist. She always puts butter on it so you'd better grab one of my paper napkins."

Pete hadn't been offered a slice of home-made cake for years. His wife was always trying out new diets – salad based, no carbs. She didn't bake anything. As other colleagues went home to wives or partners, he sat alone, in the canteen, it was the only way to get a hot meal. Chips with everything – no wonder he was putting on weight! He smiled to himself; there were some aspects of Angela's personality that would *not* be missed!

The ginger cake went down a treat. Sophie's mum was a good cook and if she was anything like her daughter, she'd have a warm, pleasing personality.

Two days later, Buxton and Hollis caught the eleven-forty-five train to London; this time they were due to meet Desiree, but not until two o'clock. Would she be able to throw any light on the situation? They must tread carefully, be polite and make no insinuations, after all, there was no proof of an affair, merely idle gossip.

Sophie sat quietly, reading a fashion magazine. Buxton was mulling things over, trying to organise his thoughts into some sort of order.

It was more than six weeks since Rupert's disappearance. Desiree's nerves would be in shreds, even more so if they were in a loving relationship. Thank goodness she didn't live alone. At least she could 'open up' and talk to her cousin, Rosina; it was good keep it in the family.

Buxton nodded his head, yes, Desiree will have worked it out, she's an intelligent young lady. Rupert must have been kidnapped, nothing else made sense. Perhaps one of London's criminal gangs was hoping for a huge ransom. The Gilbys were a wealthy family; they'd earned their *celebrity status*, a fact which made them a sitting target…

Roxy had been as cool as a cucumber. "He'll be back," she kept saying. "Perhaps he's having some sort of mid-life crisis. He loves the Maldives – may I suggest you make enquires at all the five-star hotels? Oh, you might like to have a word with David Fanshawe, see if Rupert's secretary has accompanied him."

She'd chuckled. "Rupert thinks he's God's gift to women. Even so, DI Buxton, you can only take so much sun, sea and sex."

Buxton was suspicious. Shouldn't Roxy be displaying visible signs of anxiety? Perhaps she was having an affair too – their perfect marriage no more than a sham. Perhaps he was over-thinking the whole situation and Roxy hated to admit, even to herself, her husband was an adulterer. Was she still in love with him?

Deep down, Roxy might be scared witless, unable to sleep, wondering if she'd ever see her husband again. This alone, might be the reason for her sarcastic comments, dark humour and uncaring attitude.

Buxton and Hollis were in agreement, there must be no mention of kidnapping, or ransom being paid. They were here, in London, to discuss Rupert's disappearance, nothing else. Hugo and Alicia had paid the ransom, but no-one else was aware of the kidnapping, not even Roxy, although the Dawsons had been told it was a distinct possibility. Sometimes, it's best to keep your cards close to your chest; the less people know the better, and the greater the chance someone will drop themselves in it…

No-one would say David Fanshawe was an attractive man; even less so when nervous, sweaty and flushed. For some members of the public a visit from the police is extremely stressful, making them look guilty, even though they've committed no wrong-doing whatsoever.

Fanshawe had been blessed with thick, wiry eyebrows; Sophie noticed a few white hairs, growing at awkward angles. She tried, but failed to ignore them – why doesn't he pluck them? His hair was dyed black and dragged across his forehead in a style that reminded her of Adolf Hitler. Fanshawe was overweight, peculiar and a complete disappointment to the pair of them. His bark was far worse than his bite – if he had one…

Sophie had been expecting to meet an attractive, sophisticated businessman. Rupert couldn't resist telling Danny (boasting, might be a better word) about the deals they'd pulled off in London and Paris and how they'd worked like demons to beat off the opposition. Multi-million-pound loans were handed out as if they were hardly worth mentioning.

When Sophie and Danny were together, they'd laughed at Rupert's exploits. Perhaps it was Fanshawe's influence and questionable behaviour that turned Rupert from a delightful young man into a greedy, money-worshipping womanizer.

Fanshawe's secretary brought in three mugs of coffee, it smelled delicious but looked very strong. Sophie added cream and sugar to her mug then Buxton's.

Fanshawe shook his head, looking tired and out of sorts. "God only knows where Rupert is – he'd better come back soon, there's papers to be signed and further meetings to attend in Paris.

"I simply don't understand it, this strange behaviour is totally out of character. He's usually so reliable and before you ask, no, his secretary hasn't run away with him. She's off sick at the moment."

"We know," replied Sophie, reassuringly, "we've already spoken to her at the flat. She was upset so she'd arranged for her cousin, Rosina, to be with her. Do you think we should encourage Desiree to come back to work? We're always told to keep busy when we're anxious…"

Fanshawe shrugged, why ask him? He couldn't care less either way. Not his problem. Desiree wasn't his secretary, he hardly knew the woman, he just paid her wages. Although, to be fair, she had a great pair of legs, especially when wearing stilettos and a short skirt…

He glared at Sophie. So many questions. D.I. Buxton doesn't say much, he just lets her prattle on, treating her as an equal when she's no more than a Detective Sergeant.

In my day, female constables were called WPCs., they knew their place, they dealt with children, shop-lifters and prostitutes, nothing else. Now they call them PCs., just like their male counterparts. I blame those television dramas, always trying to make us believe the female detectives are smarter than the men.

D.I. Buxton needs to assert his authority…

David Fanshawe looked embarrassed; he cleared his throat then addressed Buxton. "Oh, sorry, Inspector – I was miles away. I can't keep flying over to Paris, you know, my doctor says it's unwise. As you can see, I have a slight weight problem – due entirely to an under-active thyroid gland."

Sophie gazed out of the window, trying not to laugh. She'd just spotted the purple wrapper from a family-size block of Cadbury's chocolate; it was sticking out of Fanshawe's waste paper basket as if ready and eager to get him into trouble…

This was the fifth floor, what a view, no wonder Rupert loved working here so much. Good old Father Thames: grey, murky, but always full of character.

Londoners, businessmen, manual-workers and sightseers, all hurrying over Westminster Bridge, checking their watches – each one having to 'be somewhere.'

Chapter 23

Sophie tells all

Sophie swallowed a couple of paracetamol tablets, then glanced at the bedside clock, three-forty-five. Why not get up and make a cup of tea? The possibility of going back to sleep was zero. She could always read a few more pages of *Braeside Manor,* a birthday present from fellow DS., Amy Longton. "We can dream," Amy had said, with a cheeky laugh. The story was set in the Scottish Borders, a part of the world Sophie longed to visit. The main character and owner of Braeside Manor, Hamish Alexander Beaufort, was the sort of man most women found desirable. He was wealthy, handsome, athletic and more to the point, available. However, being a detective, Sophie's suspicions were aroused before she'd finished reading the first chapter. Hamish had no alibi for the night of the fire, but neither had his grumpy old butler. *"Oh, yes,"* she whispered, *"it's always the butler!"*

Sophie dragged herself back to the real world. She felt like packing a bag, jumping on a train and setting off for Scotland…

Maybe, when Rupert's kidnappers were behind bars, she'd treat her mum to a week's holiday in a country house hotel, a change of scenery would be good for both of them. Thoughts of Scotland conjured up exciting images: friendly people, small towns like Kelso (so full of atmosphere) bagpipes, castles, lochs, and fabulous scenery. Maybe she'd bump into a few rugged, bearded Scotsmen in kilts or tight jodhpurs. Hagis? Sophie chuckled, um, perhaps I'll give it a miss…

Sophie was quiet as a mouse, managing to avoid the stair that had a tendency to creak. She didn't want to disturb her mother, why should they both be deprived of sleep?

If Buxton hadn't been in a foul mood on the day Hugo Gilby left £75,000 next to the post-box, she'd have told him, there and then, she'd wanted to get it off her chest. She'd started to tell him, but he'd cut her off, saying,

'And you're telling me because?' Huh, such a pig-ignorant response!

She should have insisted and replied, *'Why don't you shut up and listen? You might learn something!'* Sophie was feeling guilty, she'd let her emotions get in the way. Her boss needed to know exactly what she'd seen at the Gilby's party. The party had been arranged by Alicia to celebrate Rupert's success in the local by-election. How splendid, her son, the new Member of Parliament for Bexhill-on-sea and Pevensey Bay. Quite an achievement for a young man with zero experience in the world of politics.

However, as the saying goes, *'It's not what you know, but who you know, that counts.'*

The date chosen by Alicia, July 15th, coincided nicely with Roxy's birthday. It still hurt when Sophie pictured Danny and Roxy together. How could she forget? *Lady in Red* was playing softly in the background. Perhaps it wasn't the most romantic of settings, behind the garden shed, but when a shaft of moonlight fell upon the couple and she witnessed their kiss, it was something beautiful, touching, but incredibly painful to watch. Sophie sighed and whispered, "If only Danny had kissed *me* in that way…"

She must tell Buxton, immediately. Would she be deployed elsewhere simply because she was Danny's ex-girlfriend? No, surely not.

Sophie frowned. Danny wasn't Roxy's type; was she merely toying with him, leading him on, having fun? Roxy was drawn to wealthy men, self-indulgent men. The sort of men who always look immaculate and make her feel alive, yet at the same time, vulnerable. In other words, men like Rupert!

Rupert Gilby and Daniel Dawson were at opposite ends of the spectrum: perhaps, for Roxanne, that was the attraction. In Sophie's opinion, Danny was good-looking, trustworthy, sensitive and honest, much like his father, Fred. At times, Danny seemed a little shy, but for some ladies, that was an endearing quality.

After Buxton finally set aside ten minutes to sit down and listen to Sophie's important piece of information – it was back to work as if nothing of importance had been discussed. However, he'd been surprisingly empathetic and almost fatherly towards her.

"I was wondering, Guv, shouldn't we be carrying out observations? After all, we haven't carried out any obs. since the afternoon we waited for the ransom to be collected."

Buxton shook his head, looking guilty. "Yes, and the less said about that the better, I made a mess of everything; thanks for not dropping me in it. I was going through a bad patch, even so, that's no excuse for the way I handled things, or the way I spoke to you. I'm really, very sorry…"

"That's alright, sir, I assumed you weren't always such an argumentative bugger."

Buxton looked across, then smiled. "Okay, Sophie, you've made you point – don't push your luck. Friends?"

Sophie nodded. "Course we are, sir."

Buxton looked serious. "Right, I assume you're referring to Roxy's house, the *Cherry Orchard*? Yeah, I was thinking the same thing.

"Since the Dawsons moved to their new bungalow in Little Common – just a few minutes' walk from Roxy's place – Danny could be with her all night, couldn't he? With no car in the driveway, no-one would be any the wiser. His parents wouldn't mention it either, would they? Now I know exactly what happened at the party, it's worth following up. Roxy isn't the sort of lady who sleeps around; she's stunning, she could have any man she wants. If she fancies Danny, it'll be commitment, on her part, not a one-night stand. If she divorces Rupert, her standard of living will plummet. She has her modelling career, of course, but for how much longer?

"Danny makes a good living out of the garden centre, yes, but don't forget, the profits will be split two ways – him and his parents."

"Blimey, sir, you've really thought this through, haven't you? If they get divorced, Roxy will have to sell the house, that would break her heart. After driving a convertible BMW, she couldn't cope with an ordinary car like mine. Roxanne expects to have the best of everything."

Buxton nodded. "Yes, she sure does. Do you think the kidnapping could be no more than a smokescreen? That postman, driving off like a maniac, he must be involved, perhaps he's working for the pair of 'em! I wonder, did Roxy pay some villain to collect the ransom, then murder her husband? I've seen it all before; it wouldn't be cheap, but there's always someone prepared to commit murder if the price is right. When I divorce Angela, I'll get half of everything. Roxy might not be prepared to settle for half, not if she can get the lot!"

"Well, it's certainly food for thought, Guv. If Danny is crazy about her – who knows what he might do?" She chuckled. "It's a pity we can't borrow your wife's bright green car: has she taken it with her?"

Buxton sighed, then, to her surprise, chuckled. "Yeah, course she has, Sophie. What about your Fiesta? Let's go to the other extreme, a bland looking motor, silver-grey. You've only had it a few months, Danny won't be aware of it. Remember when you went to the Dawson's place, to interview Danny? You took a CID car. We'll park opposite *The Cherry Orchard,* see if Roxy gets any other male visitors, although it's highly unlikely. No doubt we'll catch young Mr Dawson sneaking up the driveway…"

"If it's late, sir, can we take fish and chips with us? Being on obs., is *so* boring, we'll need something to cheer us up."

Buxton nodded. "Yeah, like it – nice idea. I think that could be arranged, on expenses.

"Did you say you enjoyed running? Well, perhaps I'll join you, one day – I've put on twelve pounds since the wife left. I'll need to buy a new track-suit, the old one is a little on the tight side."

Sophie laughed. "Do you know, sir, I had a track-suit like that – far too tight. Silly me, I thought it'd shrunk in the wash, until the day I weighed myself…"

Chapter 24

A watertight alibi

Pete Buxton belched, loudly, then apologised, blaming the fish and chips. He checked his watch: ten-fifty-five. "Shall we call it a day? It's highly unlikely he'll turn up now. The garden centre closes at six, he's not going to sit at home twiddling his thumbs. Do you realize, we've been here since seven-thirty?"

Sophie winced. "No wonder my bum's numb. It's all the sitting around. Still, I enjoyed the fish and chips; same again tomorrow, sir?"

Buxton smiled. "Yeah, why not? 'The Happy Plaice' has dozens of five-star reviews, *'The best fish and chips in East Sussex.'* Can't say fairer than that. I agree, lovely crispy batter."

"I'm gonna stretch my legs, if that's okay with you, Guv, just up to the second lamppost and back. Keep your eyes peeled!"

Sophie walked briskly towards the first lamppost, looking round as she walked – she hadn't given up yet. It was a quiet night, no-one about, not even dog-walkers. Suddenly, a dark figure appeared, hurrying towards Roxy's house, she caught her breath, it was Danny! Seconds later, he nipped through the wrought-iron gate that leads to the back garden from where Rupert had been abducted. Sophie nodded, of course, there'd be no need for Roxy to open the electric gates to let Danny in, he could walk straight through. She rushed back to the car. "That was lucky, good job we waited! Did you see him?"

"You bet I did," replied Buxton, rubbing his hands together. "and it's a good job you decided to stretch your legs, otherwise we'd have driven off and missed him!"

The following day, Buxton and Hollis made an unannounced visit to Dawson's Garden Centre, hoping to catch Danny unawares.

Danny looked annoyed rather than uncomfortable. "I suppose you'd better come through to the office. Dad won't be here until this afternoon, he's been invited to an open day – that new garden centre, close to Battle Abbey.

They've employed dad as an advisor – huh, my father, a consultant? Still, last year's takings were up again, so he must be doing something right. They're calling it *The Abbey Garden Centre* – dad's idea. The owners wanted to call it *William the Conqueror's Garden centre* – oh my God, can you believe it? What a mouthful, especially if you're answering the phone. To be honest, I don't think William the Conqueror did a lot of gardening!" Danny looked across at Sophie and winked.

Even though they'd received a friendly wave from Jenny Dawson (busy opening up the café) Danny didn't ask if they'd like a coffee.

Once Buxton sat down and started to ask a few unexpected questions, Danny's attitude changed; his replies became snappy and at times, downright rude.

"Yes, we're having an affair, *so what?* Roxy and I have been seeing each other for months, besides, since Rupert disappeared, she's a nervous wreck, someone has to look after her. And in case you haven't worked it out already, Rupert is having an affair with Desiree, his secretary, she works at Fanshawe and Peabody, *not* the House of Commons. Okay? Happy now?"

Sophie was shocked: this wasn't the Danny Dawson with whom she'd fallen in love – why was he being so rude, so aggressive? Maybe he was being defensive. He'd never been in trouble with the law, yet here he was being questioned about the disappearance of his lover's husband – it didn't look good...

Danny stared at his lap-top and nodded. "Ah, here it is. Rupert disappeared on the 17th – is that right? We all worked late that evening, mum, dad, me and Elsie Lovage, a well overdue stock-take. Since the failed kidnap attempt, we've taken Elsie home, right up to her front-door, a promise made by my dad. There's no shortage of volunteers, it's only four miles and everybody loves Elsie."

Danny frowned. "Oh, hang on a minute, I didn't drive Elsie home, no, Tom Evans did. He's Elsie's partner, smashing bloke, they're made for each other. Yes, I remember now, he stayed to give us a hand with the stock-take and he's been working for us ever since – part-time, same as Elsie. Anyway, like I said, we were all here until after ten."

Danny was getting annoyed, he resented Buxton's probing questions so he attempted to turn the tables. He too had a right to ask questions, although there was no guarantee he'd get any coherent answers.

"I assume there's still no news? It's not like Rupert, he loves being in the limelight. What about his job at the bank? He keeps telling us how valuable he is. What's going on at Westminster then, who's taking care of Rupert's constituents? I think Roxy's right, something terrible must have happened to him, nothing else makes sense."

As they drove away, Buxton frowned. "As alibis go, that would take some beating. I hope you agree, Sophie, I *had* to tell Danny about the kidnapping, he needed to know, didn't he? He *insisted,* he must be the one to explain everything to Roxy, you know, about Hugo handing over the £75,000. I did offer. Perhaps it's better coming from him.

"Well, it wasn't a wasted visit, was it? At least we can cross Roxy and Danny of our 'persons of interest' list. Another thing, it's time to authorize a press-release: brief, but to the point. Something like this:

'*Rupert Gilby, the recently elected M.P. for Bexhill-on-sea and Pevensey Bay, has been kidnapped and the ransom paid. I regret to say, despite making extensive enquiries, we are unable to find any clues as to his whereabouts. We can only hope he's safe and well and will be released, very soon.*'

"Unfortunately, Sophie, ninety-nine times out of a hundred, once the kidnappers have collected the ransom, it's 'Goodnight Vienna,' as the saying goes. Sorry to be flippant but I doubt we'll be seeing Rupert Gilby again. Need I say, I'd like nothing more than to be proved wrong? Murder is easy, but disposing of the body?" Buxton shook his head, "That's the tricky part. We'll carry on with our enquiries and see how things pan out…"

"Something's been needling me, sir, the attempted kidnapping of Elsie Lovage. We've said it before, but it *has* to be connected, doesn't it? Some sort of trial run. Rupert has a price on his head: wealthy family, trophy wife, celebrity life style and all that jazz, but Elsie? A lady in her seventies, widowed, works at a garden centre, no money or family to speak of – let's face it – who the hell would pay the ransom? I wonder, how much is Elsie worth? She's priceless to the Dawsons and her friends, but in reality, five grand? That sounds heartless, I know, but you get my drift."

Back in the office, Buxton put his feet on the desk; he was feeling depressed. He opened a packet of chocolate digestives, six were placed on top of a pile of paperwork. Sophie leaned over and grabbed a biscuit, just the one, she had a different relationship with food.

Buxton knew, after thirty years in the job, he'd become cynical; he'd seen so much pain, suffering and downright evil. You had to harden your heart otherwise you couldn't cope. He smiled, Sophie still possessed a naïve, but delightful enthusiasm for the job, he hoped she'd never change…

He ran his fingers through his greying hair. Perhaps, if he'd followed a different path and become 'safe but boring,' working nine to five in a cosy office, his marriage would have turned out to be a happy one. Would Angela have changed her mind and stopped taking the contraceptive pill? If so, they'd probably have children of their own. Now, less than a year from his retirement, he should be feeling excited. They should be living together, planning exotic holidays and romantic weekends away; they could certainly afford it. Pete tried not to dwell on the subject – *it was too painful*…

As a young DI, he'd been hoping for a challenging case, something to get his teeth into: a bank robbery, a kidnapping or the arrest of an infamous drug dealer, a *Mr Big,* yes, something rewarding. Perhaps, one day, there'd be further promotion, *Detective Chief Inspector Buxton.* He used to smile, um, sounds good to me!

However, when a murder was committed, just six months after being promoted to DI, reality struck home: suddenly, he felt the weight of the world upon his shoulders. What would happen if he mislaid a vital piece of evidence or failed to 'join the dots?' The killer might never be traced! What if the killer was arrested, then charged, but found *not guilty* by the jurors?

Every year, Buxton and his wife longed for a relaxing, uninterrupted Christmas Day – always spent at his brother's house – five miles away in the village of Little Drayford. Was it really too much to ask? On this particular occasion, Angela had smiled and said, "Fingers crossed, love, let's hope you don't get called out."

Pete had been telephoned at mid-day; he'd been having a good time, playing Monopoly with his young nephews.

The body of Sarah-Jane Smith had just been discovered, after six weeks of fruitless searching. She'd been hidden amongst the tall bracken (brown and decayed now until the following spring) at the far end of Arundel golf course. A young golden retriever had become excited and barked loudly until his owner joined him to discover what all the fuss was about…

Derrick Cassidy was a golfer but not a good one. However, he was aware of a muddy area, surrounded by trees and far away from the well-trodden footpath. As it had a tendency to flood, the area was of no interest to the golf club and therefore ignored by the groundsmen. Even a novice golfer, with a handicap of thirty-six, would be shocked if a golf ball landed this far from the green. Recently, a notice board had been attached to a nearby sycamore tree, stating: *Out of Bounds.*

It'd taken over a year to pin-down the killer of twelve-year-old schoolgirl, Sarah-Jane Smith. Unfortunately, Cassidy's best friend had given him what appeared to be a rock-solid alibi.

At five o'clock on that autumnal evening, just as Sarah-Jane was hurrying back from the local convenience store, the heavens opened. Her mother could think of no other reason why her daughter would have accepted a lift from a complete stranger. A CCTV camera, half a mile from Sarah-Jane's home, had revealed a white transit van (with a cracked headlight) driving slowly alongside her. Despite the weather, the number plate was clear enough to be used in evidence. Sarah-Jane, shielded by the van, had turned into the Greenford Estate, a run-down part of town with a bad reputation. Sarah-Jane had promised to visit her new friend, Rachel, who lived in one of the large blocks of flats; she'd call round after five o'clock. Her mother had told her to come straight home, she must *not* visit her friend – the Greenford Estate was a 'no go' area, out of the question. However, Rachel was welcome to visit their house whenever she liked. Besides, the bacon and eggs were needed for the evening's meal. The only other camera in the area failed to picked up any helpful images. As Sarah-Jane failed to arrive at Rachel's home, it was highly likely she'd climbed or been dragged into the van.

Derrick Cassidy stood in the dock, looking pleased with himself – grinning in the direction of Sarah-Jane's family. He pleaded not guilty, but as with many cases, DNA proved beyond any reasonable doubt, he was the killer of an innocent young school girl. The chances of the murderer being anyone else were a billion to one.

The foreman of the jury looked directly at the judge when he replied in a loud, confident voice, *"Guilty!"* At last, Buxton's team could relax.

When the judge handed down a life sentence, with a minimum term of twenty years behind bars – Buxton was furious. Cassidy was a monster. The sentence wasn't long enough, life should mean life. Cassidy was nineteen, if he was released, aged thirty-nine, would he stalk another pretty young girl, drag her into his van and kill again? You bet he would…

Although Pete Buxton tried hard to forget that particular Christmas Day, it was impossible: it had been like no other…

As he left his brother's house, he'd turned and smiled. 'Sorry about this, folks – I hope I won't be too long. Now then, you lot, leave me some turkey, plenty of white meat – I don't like the grey stuff. Oh, and don't go nicking all the cranberry sauce and gravy!"

He'd tried to look cheerful, gazing at his loved ones, sitting round the table, pulling crackers and wearing paper hats as they waited patiently for their Christmas dinner. He left the house with the smell of turkey and roast potatoes wafting round the kitchen – his stomach began to rumble.

Poor Angela: she'd been the life and soul of any party. She'd enjoyed helping out with the cooking, looking after their much-loved nephews, never complaining, never knowing when her husband might return…

Pete's demanding career had taken over his life, pushing her into the background, making her feel like a stranger. Life had changed her, and not for the better.

Perhaps a new life in Newcastle, with her sister, was just what she needed…

Chapter 25

A worrying phone call

Joseph answered the telephone: his face lit up. Yes, of course he remembered the delightful, but nervous, Miss Nancy Musgrove.

"Ah, and how are you, dear lady?" he enquired, his voice as soft as silk…

Her face became hot, her cheeks pink. She'd forgotten about Joseph's big brown eyes and his warm, welcoming, Irish accent. "Oh, erm, yes, I'm fine thank you, Mr O'Reilly."

Nancy tried to sound like a prim, virginal, 1950s school teacher: her pretty hair transformed by a tight, curly perm. She could visualise herself wearing a beige twin-set with a brown, tweed skirt, finishing, tastefully, well below the knee.

It might be wise, safer perhaps, to give the impression she was a lady with no interest whatsoever in men. The O'Reilly brothers' effortless charm and rugged good looks made her feel uncomfortable. They were crude, earthy, uneducated and in need of a lengthy soak in a bath full of scented bubbles! Despite their numerous failings, Nancy found Joseph extremely attractive, worryingly so, she felt ashamed of her feelings towards him. She cleared her throat, then continued.

"Now then, Mr O'Reilly, regarding my previous visit to your smallholding. I informed you and your brother, at the time, that a regular check must be carried out in order to continue with your *'Site of Special Scientific Interest'* status and relevant grant. There is no laid-down timescale, but we feel a visit, every two or three years, is not unreasonable. We appear to have overlooked the last visit – I do apologise, I must have mislaid the paperwork. All I can find is the agreement made with the previous occupiers, Bert and Olive Renton.

"There'll be no need to disturb you. I remember the location of the field, so I'm more than happy to walk round unaccompanied. I'm sure I'll be less than an hour. I assume the purple 'angel wing' orchids *are* in flower? I thought it wise to wait until the end of May, just to be on the safe side. Would it be convenient if I called in one afternoon this week?"

"There's nothing I'd like more," replied Joseph. "Me and Paddy have nothing planned this week, nothing at all. Those purple orchids are in full bloom – tis a sight for sore eyes. You'll enjoy walking round the field, it'll do you a power of good. Fancy being shut in an office, day after day, tis a cruel thing – I couldn't be doing with it. Oh, will you be wanting to photograph the orchids?"

Nancy laughed, "Yes, I will, of course I will – for our records. Anyway, it'll be sometime after three. I'll be driving down from Reading, so it depends on the traffic."

"Okay. Goodbye to yer, Miss Musgrove."

"Now then, Paddy, me boy, we have a slight problem. The lovely Miss Musgrove will be coming to see us one afternoon this week…

"Yes, she'll be walking round the edge of our field, photographing the orchids. I must say, they're looking grand. Surely, she'll have no reason to look elsewhere, will she?"

Paddy frowned, "No, course not."

Joseph felt reassured, he smiled. "Rupert's safe and sound at the top end of the field, under the sycamore tree, well away from any nosy parkers. We've checked that piece of ground, over and over, there are no signs of disturbed earth. By the way, brother, have you noticed the poppies? They're looking beautiful, a sea of red, blowing gently in the wind. Fancy them growing right over Rupert's grave. He'd like that. Folks sneer at us, but we're clever, very clever, we know what we're doing. *No-one will ever find his body; I can promise you that…*"

Life was good and the O'Reillys intended to make the most of it. Joseph opened another bottle of Irish whiskey. Kidnapping, stealing a Royal Mail van, even murder – not a problem for them. The police hadn't a clue, they were useless. Patrick turned on the television. "Let's watch another episode of *Only Fools and Horses*. Great characters, I love that Del Boy, he's always up to something, just like us."

Nothing could be further from the truth…

Joseph looked towards Paddy and scowled. "Come on, will yer – hurry up, pass the pickled eggs, I'm starving. Do you know something? Just thinking about Miss Musgrove has given me quite an appetite. Her jeans were very tight, did you notice? Such a lovely firm bottom: I felt like grabbing hold of it."

Patrick laughed and winked at his brother, of course he'd noticed her tight jeans. Miss Musgrove moved like an angel…

He frowned. Perhaps they should have kidnapped Nancy instead of Rupert – but not for financial gain. No, they'd tie her up and keep her in the barn, forever. She would be their plaything. He shivered at the very thought of it.

Melanie, the young lady who worked in Halfords, had turned down Joseph's proposal of marriage, despite being taken out for a pub meal and given a huge bouquet of red roses. How ungrateful. Even more surprising, she'd refused an invitation to stay the night, in Joseph's bed!

Oh, well, at least she'd provided them with a pair of shiny new number plates for the Royal Mail van…

Chapter 26

A surprise development

Buxton looked as if he had the weight of the world on his shoulders. "You look deep in thought, sir."

He sighed. "Yeah, tell me about it. We need to go back to square one, Sophie, there's no alternative, we're making no progress at all. Someone must have seen something, no matter how insignificant it seemed at the time. It could be the key to finding Rupert: alive or dead.

"We'll knock on a few more doors. We didn't speak to everyone on our last visit. Some were out, some were at work and a few were on holiday. We'll begin further down the road, then work our way back towards the Gilby's house."

George Hanson, a retired insurance broker, lived at number nineteen. Although in his mid-eighties he was still sharp as a knife. When he realized they were police officers, he apologized for not inviting them inside for a cup of tea. "I've been in the garden all afternoon – what I need now is a damn good shower. Awfully sorry."

Sophie laughed. "No problem, sir, we won't keep you long. We're just making enquiries to see if anyone, down this end of the road, saw anything out of the ordinary on the day Mr Gilby disappeared. You may have seen a recent press release or spotted DI Buxton on the local television news."

Mr Hanson scratched his head. "Only the red van, yes, something peculiar going on there…

"Well, I was just about to take the dog for a walk, no idea what time it was. Sorry. My wife had made a chicken curry, so I wanted some exercise before tucking in! You should never take a walk on a full stomach, very bad for you.

"Anyway, as I crossed the road, to get to the bridleway, I noticed a Royal Mail van, parked opposite the Gilby's house. Two dodgy looking types, just sitting there, doing absolutely nothing.

"I had to smile, no windows were open, it looked bloody smoky inside! Ah, I remember now, both chaps had dark hair. At the time, I thought it rather odd, you know, neither man wearing a postman's uniform. When I got back, thirty minutes later, the van was still there.

"Obviously, at my age, one doesn't like to get involved, the men might have turned nasty. I should've contacted the police, but to be honest, it completely slipped my mind. As my wife said at the time – *probably something and nothing.*"

Buxton looked up and smiled. "You'd be surprised, sir, a small nugget of information, like yours, can turn out to be very helpful. It's rather like a jigsaw puzzle and you've given us another piece. Many Thanks. Oh, Mr Hanson, make sure you have a long, relaxing shower. *You've earned it...*"

Mr Hanson laughed, nodded and waved before shutting the front door.

Brayfield House, built in 1935, was an imposing dwelling; five bedrooms, large garden with pond and a decent size swimming pool. Although a few doors down from *The Cherry Orchard,* and on the opposite side of the road, it had a good clear view of the Gilby's house, driveway and part of their front garden.

Lorraine Burchell was alone when Buxton and Hollis rang the doorbell. She yawned and gazed out of the bay window. A middle-aged man and a young lady, what the hell do they want? She shook her head, I hope they're not Jehovah's Witnesses, they make my blood boil. "Yes?" she said, sharply, opening the front door no wider than was necessary.

Buxton explained their reason for calling and apologized if it was inconvenient. Mrs Burchell smiled warmly, the Detective Inspector had nice manners, that was a good start. "No, it's not inconvenient, do come in."

Mrs Burchell was an accountant, working from home. "My eyes are usually focused on my lap top, although I do get up to stretch my legs. I look out of the window, frequently – although there's rarely anything going on! Oh, I wonder, would you care for a cup of tea?"

Buxton and Hollis smiled, oh, yes please; they'd not had a drink since lunch-time. As Lorraine Burchell busied herself in the kitchen, her son arrived home from school. He stared at them, 'Who are you?" he asked, rudely.

Buxton laughed: cheeky devil. The boy looked at them inquisitively, then nodded his head. "Oh, I see – detectives, are you? Well, I saw something very odd that day. I bet no-one else noticed. D'you wanna know about it?"

"Yes, please," replied Sophie, although she was thinking, for goodness-sake get on with it.

Fourteen-year-old Toby Burchell opened a can of coke, spilling some on the dark coloured carpet; he rubbed it in with his foot. After drinking the rest of it, he belched, then laughed. Buxton smiled, *"Come on, lad, get on with it, please."*

"Well, it's like this. I saw that Roxanne woman going out in her new car, a convertible BMW. It must have cost a fortune! She looked fantastic, always does." He blushed. "All my mates fancy her. Anyway, she was on her own.

No, sorry, she wasn't. I forgot, that dog, Winston, was with her, sitting in the back.

"Just after she left, I went round to Jordan's house, he lives down the road, number thirty-seven. There was a Royal Mail van parked outside our house, for ages. Two blokes were sitting inside. They looked like a couple of crims to me! They weren't postmen, no way. They weren't even wearing a uniform."

Mrs Burchell returned, carrying a large tray with three mugs of tea, a sugar bowl and a flowery saucer piled high with ginger nut biscuits.

"Oh, yes, our Toby mentioned the red van when he came back from Jordan's house, about twenty minutes later. I went upstairs and looked out of my bedroom window. The men were still sitting in the van, doing nothing.

"Our mail is delivered between ten o'clock and mid-day, no later than that. Geoff Palmer is ever so nice; best postman we've ever had. Keeps an eye on the elderly, too. That wasn't his van, oh no, it was filthy. Geoff would *never* drive something in that state."

Mrs Burchell looked uncomfortable; if only she'd jotted down the number plate.

"Go on, Toby, tell the detectives what you saw next."

"Yeah, okay, mum – give us a break!

"Well, the red van was driven across the road to the MPs house, it parked next to the sideway. I couldn't see much from my bedroom window, only the front of it, cos it'd been reversed in, like. Anway, after a while, I saw it drive off, quite fast. That's it – end of."

Toby stood up and shrugged. "I'm going to my bedroom now – homework to do."

Sophie looked him in the eye. "That's extremely helpful, Toby, the best news we've had all week. We'll need a written statement, of course, but there's no mad rush."

Buxton and Hollis sat together drinking their mugs of strong tea, this time in Bexhill's antiquated police station. The previous month a few portacabins had arrived – then, out of the blue and to everyone's relief, an announcement had been made. The following spring, the foundations for a brand-new Police station (on the outskirts of town) would be laid. A loud cheer and a round of applause was heard coming from the CID office…

The canteen was built in the Victorian era, as part of the original structure: now, it was in desperate need of some TLC. Mavis, the cook, made exceptionally good chips; golden brown and always piping hot. She insisted, she must have Maris Piper potatoes, nothing else would do. "Here we are, sweetheart!" she shouted, nodding towards Sophie, "Double egg and chips for two."

"Oh, I'm going to enjoy this," said her boss, "pass the brown sauce, please. All in all, we've had a very productive day. Tomorrow, all we have to do is find out where the van was stolen from and who the hell was driving it! At least it confirms what we already knew, the speeding Royal Mail van *did* pick up the ransom."

Sophie showered, ate two Weetabix, drove to work, then turned on her computer. It was almost seven-thirty. Five minutes later,

Buxton arrived. He yawned. Sophie stifled a giggle; he looked as if he'd been dragged through a hedge backwards. Even so, if he had a decent haircut and smartened himself up, he'd be quite a catch!

Pete handed her a latte, from Joe's café, opposite the police station. Mavis made great chips and she could fry anything to perfection but until they supplied her with a good quality coffee machine, Joe's café would be every detective's first choice.

There was nowhere better after a long night, or an early start…

Sophie checked her watch, three-thirty; she had a tension headache. Two paracetamol tablets were eased out of their foil wrapper. "D'you want a couple, Guv?" she enquired.

"Yeah, why not? Let's live dangerously," he replied, with a little chuckle. "If you've got a headache, you ought to go home – you've been here over eight hours. Maybe you could do with some fresh air?

"I wonder – and if it's not presumptuous on my part – would madam care to accompany me to the seafront? We'll park up then take a brisk walk to the De La Warr pavilion. That sea-breeze is just the thing for banishing a headache. We can go in the restaurant and order something light, like a chicken salad. No more chips for a few days, eh? It'll be my treat, how about it? I'd be glad of the company."

"That would be lovely, sir, and you did ask in a very gentlemanly way. *You can be charming, you know, when you want to…*

"The thing is, Guv, I promised mum I'd take her out for something to eat, unless – well, could we pick her up? I'll ring her first, it's so early, she won't be expecting me home before five."

"Yes, of course she can come with us, I'd like to meet this mother of yours. I know one thing – she makes a great ginger cake…"

Sophie plumped up her pillow then put it behind her back. Her book, *Braeside Manor*, was on the bedside table. She removed the small piece of torn paper she'd been using as a bookmark. She chuckled. "Oh, fancy that. Well, who's a naughty boy?" Hamish Beaufort *did* have an alibi for the night of the fire! He'd been with Annabel Duncan, the vicar's flame-haired wife – all night long. Sophie smiled. That's a clever twist, good luck to the pair of them. Annabel's husband, Roderick, twenty years her senior, sounded very boring. Who wouldn't be tempted to spend the night with the sexy Laird of Braeside Manor?

After less than fifteen minutes, the book was returned to the bedside table. Sophie finished her mug of hot chocolate.

It was no good, she couldn't concentrate. Her head was all over the place. She'd read one line three times and it still didn't register…

She shook her head; you couldn't make it up! Her mother and Pete Buxton, behaving as if they'd known each other for years. There was definitely a spark between them, her mother's cheeks had become quite pink, she didn't know whether to laugh or feel embarrassed. At least they were roughly the same age: her mum was fifty-six and Pete a mere forty-nine.

She smiled. I suppose it could have been worse. Mum didn't run off with a toy-boy, or sign up to one of those dodgy dating sites and give her entire savings to some Nigerian 'prince.'

The previous week her mother had received a bizarre message on her Facebook page; it was lengthy, badly composed and contained no punctuation whatsoever. It was supposedly from a five-star General, in the U.S. army, Chuck Theodore Mason, a man who claimed to have fallen in love with her mother's photograph.

He'd written: *'Next to Eve, you are the most beautiful woman in the world.'* Sophie winced – cringeworthy. She'd made her mother delete the message, immediately. In reality, it'd been sent by a Columbian woman, a mother of six, part of a gang, trawling through the profiles of middle-aged British women…

Sophie closed her eyes. If mum can find a nice, trustworthy man, so can I. It's a big world; there must be someone out there who fancies me! All I want is a man who's warm, supportive and willing to share my likes and dislikes. Yeah, good looking too…

Within minutes, she'd fallen into a deep, relaxing sleep.

Chapter 27

A pleasing response

"You're looking flushed, sir. Anything wrong?"

"No, I'm fine, thanks, Sophie. I'm just hoping we get a good response to our latest press release. You never know, we might get some information on a stolen Royal Mail van. Now we have coherent statements from George Hanson, Toby Birchell and his mum, I'm feeling good, we're making progress, at last."

"Well, I've just received some info that'll make you stop and think. Guess what? *It's about the theft of a Royal Mail van.* I had a phone call from a D.S. Laura Jarvis, Hampshire police, Basingstoke area. She told me about one of their unsolved murders, it's appalling. They are really struggling – absolutely nothing to go on. Perhaps we can help each other...

"Here goes. A fifty-six-year-old postman was making his last delivery of the day, Glebe farm, down the end of a remote country lane. He might have been followed, we'll never know, or perhaps someone was waiting for him. Anyway, he was beaten up so badly, he died from a massive stroke. As Laura Jarvis said, this is murder, it has to be, although it probably wasn't their intention to kill him, just shut him up, put him out of action for a while. The postman, Bob Higgins, was fit as a fiddle, no health problems at all – the previous month he'd run the London Marathon in under five hours. That tells you, they must have given him one hell of a beating. Poor bloke.

"Basingstoke police dealt with a similar case, the previous month. Another postie, Dave Prentis, was beaten up, all his parcel were stolen. However, the van wasn't touched.

"I may be wrong but something tells me these two incidents are not connected.

"Bob Higgins was found by the farmer, lying in the lane, dead. No sign of his red van. It was assumed his van was nicked for obvious reasons, to steal the contents. Bit odd though, waiting until the postie's making his last delivery of the day – wouldn't it be better to nick the van when it was full of stuff? I wouldn't be surprised if it was Rupert's kidnappers! Clever move, stealing a Royal Mail van. Hiding in plain sight, as the saying goes. We know it was them, parked outside the school, opposite the post-box. No genuine postman would behave in such a way, driving off like a maniac. Outside a school, when the kids were coming out? *No way.* One of the men was sitting inside the van, engine turned on, ready to go, whilst his mate ran across the road and picked up the ransom."

"Well done, Sophie, I'm impressed. It all sounds plausible to me. *Who the hell are these geezers?* Are they London-based, or do they come from Hampshire? I always assumed they were local, you know, Sussex villains. They certainly knew Rupert and Roxy's address.

"Perhaps they stole the van, then, because they'd killed the driver, they had to clone a number plate from another Royal Mail van – yes, that would make sense. Check out the number plates issued to similar vans in East Sussex, see what you can find. Unfortunately, we've only got part of it – KW62 – still, better than nothing…"

Sophie nodded. "Will do, sir. I'm still confused. We've always assumed the kidnappers had a grudge against Rupert, you know, someone he'd upset. I never felt they'd kidnapped him just for the money. Then there's Elsie Lovage, we're convinced she was their 'trial run.' If, not, what the hell were they playing at?"

Buxton nodded. "Well, I'm ruling nothing out. We must consider every possibility. This is by far the most complicated case I've ever worked on. Never fear, we'll get there in the end, we usually do.

"Oh, by the way, you'll be getting your own meal this evening, I'm taking your mum out for a curry!" He supressed a laugh.

Sophie frowned. "Oh, great, thanks Guv, something to look forward to. I'll think of you both, enjoying your delicious spicy meals while I sit alone, weeping, eating stale bread and mouldy cheese, washed down with a glass of tap water. Yeah – but on the other hand, perhaps I'll pick up a bottle of Sauvignon Blanc, from New Zealand, then I can drown my sorrows."

"When I retire, *Miss Hollis,* some poor devil will be promoted to DI. I wonder, are you ready?" He smirked. "Don't worry, girl, I'm only teasing, you'll be my number one choice."

Chapter 28

Nancy conquers her fears

Nancy Musgrove had promised to visit the O'Reilly brothers, she couldn't wriggle out of it. It was her job to keep an eye on them. She must ensure the *Site of Special Scientific Interest* was kept exactly as nature intended. Although she was loathe to admit it, she was dreading what seemed like an ordeal rather than a pre-arranged meeting. The mere thought of sitting in their squalid kitchen raised her anxiety levels. There was something about the way they looked at her that sent out warning signals – yes, but why? What did she think they intended to do to her? They didn't look, or behave, like serial rapists! Although, to be fair, who does?

Admittedly, Joseph was a flirt, but no-one would call that a crime. He adored women and assumed, correctly, many found him attractive. However, few women would welcome a relationship with someone from such a murky background, a man for whom cleanliness and good hygiene were of little importance. Patrick wasn't the sharpest knife in the box, but he was harmless. She smiled; as usual, she was over-reacting. The brothers were 'all talk' they meant no harm…

Even now, years after her first visit to Woodford End, Nancy could recall the aromas that assaulted her nostrils the moment she entered Bluebell Cottage. Cheap dog food, pickled eggs, stale sweat, steaming wellington boots, a blocked sink – the list was endless.

She'd checked with Google maps: one hundred and two miles would take her to the outskirts of Hastings. The satnav would guide her a further seven miles to the tiny village of Woodford End: population four hundred and thirty-eight.

She mustn't forget to take a drink with her, plus something to eat. She'd stop at the services, but only for the loo. Queuing for food was time-consuming and not her idea of fun. Why not sit in the car, listening to music whilst enjoying a ham and tomato sandwich made by her own fair hand?

She nodded. "I'll take a packet of custard creams with me; something easy to nibble on the drive home." Crisps were too greasy.

She had a Thermos flask somewhere; it'd belonged to her much-loved father. She must check under the sink – had she put it behind the dustpan and brush? A flask full of sweet, milky coffee: yes, she could make it last all day.

A tear rolled down Nancy's cheek, she brushed it away with the back of her hand. *"Oh, dad, I miss you so much,"* she whispered…

The O'Reilly brothers appeared to enjoy making 'unusual' fillings for their sandwiches. She could remember seeing a plate, piled high, on the grubby kitchen table. God only knows what was inside them. Beetroot had been one of the fillings, its vivid colour leeching out into the thick, white bread. They'd looked hurt and disappointed when she'd refused to eat anything, drink anything, or even sit down on the sofa next to *Killer,* the dog.

Nancy checked her watch: yeah, there was plenty of time before the ten o'clock news began to send an email to cousin Robbie.

She didn't have a lot to say but he was always interested in what she was doing and where she was going. Their chosen professions had much in common, mainly, protecting the environment from idiots and liars…

Hi Robbie,

Hope you're getting over that heavy cold.

Has the fly-tipping decreased in your area? It's such a blight on the landscape. You haven't mentioned asbestos for a while; perhaps most of the Victorian buildings and brown-field sites have had it removed by experts. Let's hope so!

I'm having a trip down to East Sussex tomorrow. I forgot to tell you about the purple 'angel wing' orchids. There's an SSSI in Woodford End, a tiny village near Hastings. I'm so excited, they're in full bloom. I'll send you some photos. I'm taking some 'nosh' and a flask with me – it'll be a long day. I wouldn't even drink a cup of tea where I'm going. Honestly, Bluebell Cottage is a tip and the owners are quite scary. Hope that doesn't make me sound like a snob or a coward. Send out a search party if I don't return!

Robbie read Nancy's email, twice. He was shocked – Bluebell Cottage sounded awful; they must be a peculiar couple. No doubt they were very old and set in their ways. His amazement turned to anger – Nancy shouldn't be going there on her own – not if she's scared! Silly girl, why doesn't she take somebody with her? One of the juniors, preferably male, someone who's learning the ropes...

Woodford End, I've come across that name before, although, in connection with what? Huh, no idea. Not recently, though. It can't have been important or I'd remember the case, or at least the culprit's name. I *do* remember a huge cannabis farm, near St Leonards on sea, that's East Sussex. Good grief, that was over twenty years ago!

Robbie shook his head. "I shall be awake half the night trying to figure it out."

Chapter 29

Photographic evidence

Nancy arrived early; she could see immediately, very little had changed since her previous visit. She climbed out of her car, *Killer* (who'd developed a limp) struggled to run over and investigate. She put out her hand and stroked his head. The poor dog looked undernourished; he was tugging at her heartstrings. He sat down beside her, hoping she would make a fuss of him. Nancy searched inside her tote bag, she'd nothing for him. She unlocked the car door and reached across to the glove compartment, grabbing hold of the unopened packet of custard creams.

"Here we are, boy," she said, putting three biscuits on top of the low, partly demolished brick wall. They were eaten immediately by a grateful, but nervous animal.

The front door opened. Joseph smiled broadly.

"Well, if my eyes don't deceive me, tis Miss Nancy Musgrove. Good to see you, darlin'. I must say, you're looking fresh as a daisy.

"Paddy, come here and be quick about it. Look who's come to see us."

Paddy walked slowly to the door, a bottle of Guinness clasped in his hand; he took a long swig, then belched. He stared at Nancy, looking her up and down, his eyes resting on her breasts. She blushed. She felt frightened. What lecherous thoughts were whizzing around inside his head?

Paddy nodded. "You'd better come in then," was all he said.

"I won't, if you don't mind. I'm rather pressed for time, I've other business in the area."

The brothers looked at each other, disappointment written over their faces. Paddy scowled. They'd planned to lure Nancy into the kitchen, give her a cup of tea laced generously with vodka, then sit back and relax until she fell into a deep sleep. Joseph had promised him, once they'd carried her over to the barn, she would be theirs, forever!

Mammy's box of Oxycodone capsules was half-full; they could drug Nancy, every day, and no-one would be any the wiser. When the box was empty, Paddy would make an appointment with the empathetic, but gullible, Doctor Daphne Finch and tell her a pack of lies. He'd look miserable and say he wasn't sleeping. His back was painful too, due to his occupation; lots of heavy lifting and carrying. Chickens, ponies and pigs to feed, eggs to collect – yes, it was a hard life.

Since Mammy died, he wasn't coping. Could he have some Oxycodone capsules, please? They might make his life a little easier…

"I know what I'm gonna do!" Joseph had declared, the previous evening, "When we have her tied up in the barn, I shall telephone Nancy's office, about four-thirty – when they're waiting to go home. I shall say we're very annoyed, we've stayed in all afternoon and she hasn't turn up. It's just not good enough. Why didn't she telephone and let us know she'd changed her plans?"

Paddy's eyes had opened wide – he thought it was a brilliant idea. Joseph was a genius.

The brothers looked angry and confused. Paddy was lost for words; they had to get her into the kitchen, somehow…

Nancy repeated her question, in fact she raised her voice and pointed to the field, two hundred metres on her right.

"Is that where the orchids are, over there?"

"It is," replied Joseph, "although we'd best come with you, darlin', some of the orchids are underneath the beech hedge so they're tricky to find."

Nancy knew that arguing with them would be pointless, they would accompany her no matter how much she protested…

The orchids were incredible, a deep, yet vivid purple and larger than she'd anticipated. Some had a pure white vein running through their petals and many were still in bud. Even from afar, you could detect their waxiness.

They grew in dense clumps, much like snowdrops.

Nancy had timed her visit to perfection; she felt like an excitable schoolgirl. There were only two places in the south of England where such treasures could be found. Both had been declared a *Site of Special Scientific Interest.* No more than a handful of people knew the location of both sites; Nancy felt privileged to be one of them.

"Well, gentlemen," she said, appearing more confident than she felt, "you must be doing something right. The flowers are amazing!" She nodded. "Yes, healthy plants too, with glossy leaves."

The O'Reilly brothers grinned, looking pleased with themselves.

"I suppose they just grow here, in one small area? Nevertheless, I shall walk up to the top of the field, as far as that big sycamore tree. I'd like to stretch my legs before the long drive back to Reading. You never know, I might discover a few orchids up there!"

Joseph's attitude changed: the smile had gone, he looked irritated. *"Oh, no, Miss Nancy Musgrove – you're not going up there...*

"There are no orchids for yer by the sycamore tree. Going up there would be a waste of time. Come on now, we're going inside and you're coming with us – I'm gonna make you a nice cup of tea."

Joseph and Patrick turned their backs on her. They whistled for *Killer*, who joined them as they walked slowly along the muddy track towards Bluebell cottage.

Nancy hesitated, hoping to take a few more photographs; the last thing she wanted was to venture inside their filthy home!

At the far end of the field, in front of the sycamore tree, she'd noticed a sea of bright red poppies. They made her feel quite emotional, reminding her, almost immediately, of the First World War. Five more photographs were taken, all landscape. She put the camera away in her tote bag, hoping she'd captured the poppies in all their glory.

Suddenly, a moment of blind panic swept over her. She ran towards her car, almost tripping over the low brick wall in her attempt to escape. Something was telling her to leave Bluebell Cottage, the O'Reilly brothers, and Woodford End!

A little voice in her head was saying: *'Don't walk over to say goodbye, don't even look at them, just get in your car and drive...'*

Chapter 30

Elaine Musgrove...

Robbie Musgrove's wife, Elaine, had ceased working for Wilkins and Bramwell, the upmarket estate agency in Wallingford. Sadly, her beautiful black Mini (once considered more important than her husband) had to be returned. After a flaming row with her boss, she'd walked out and decided upon another career, something more rewarding. She was planning to take a course that would enable her to become a dental hygienist.

Although Robbie (being pragmatic) would be foolish to say sparks were flying between them and their love for one another had been rekindled, he would be more than happy to admit his wife was becoming easier to live with. Occasionally, he saw glimpses of the young woman with whom he'd fallen in love…

Being unemployed gave Elaine time for the things she'd once enjoyed, like gardening, water-colour painting, long walks in the countryside and days out, exploring her favourite Cotswold towns and villages – accompanied by her husband.

When Elaine suggested getting a small dog, Rob behaved like an excited schoolboy. "Yes! How about a Border terrier?" he'd replied.

The burgundy lipstick had been replaced by something peachy, more suited to her pale skin. Her blonde, highlighted hair – cut short and spikey – looked amazing; Robbie made a point of telling her, frequently. He hoped, in the not too-distant future, they might, *just might,* become lovers once more. As things stood, neither felt able to make the first move…

Robbie was sitting in the study, on the well-worn leather sofa, reading an email from his cousin. "Can you hear me, Elaine?" he shouted, "When you've finished watching the news, will you come through and take a look at Nancy's photographs? *They are superb."*

Elaine hurried into the room. "I've made some fresh coffee, I'll leave it on the desk, there's more room." She moved closer to her husband her eyes drawn to his lap-top.

Robbie was eager to recount Nancy's exploits. "Nancy's been down to Woodford End, East Sussex. I know she was dreading it. She mentioned a smallholding. Apparently, it has been an SSSI for many years. I imagine, by what she says, it's owned by an elderly couple and they're struggling to cope; yeah, the cottage is filthy. She didn't say much else about them, other than she'd refuse a cup of tea, even if she was gasping! Good grief, it must be bad!"

Elaine frowned. "Poor old Nancy.

"Oh, yes, those orchids are spectacular! Such a rich colour. Purple 'angel wing,' is that their name? They must be rare; I've never heard of them! Ask Nancy to print off a copy, will you? A4 size. I'll put it in a frame, in the dining room.

"East Sussex? I can remember *you* going down there, must be years ago because I'd just started working for Wilkins and Bramwell. You took the new girl with you, Emily Brown.

"There's another reason why East Sussex rings a bell, my auntie Pam lived in Bexhill, we used to stay with her during the summer holidays, she was great fun. We bought buckets and spades, fishing nets too. We'd catch tiny crabs and strange looking fish in the rock-pools. The beach is pebbly but there are a few sandy areas, when the tide goes out. There's a marvellous Art Deco place, called the De La Warr Pavilion…"

Elaine frowned when a less than pleasant memory popped into her head.

"Oh, Robbie, you kept on and on about Emily Brown. She was so pretty, so clever – I was jealous. I half expected you to leave me and move in with her. I wouldn't have blamed you; I was being a right bitch at the time."

Robbie looked sheepish. "Well, yeah, I did fancy her and our marriage was going through a rough patch, wasn't it? Nothing happened though, I promise. I think she fancied me – at the time, despite my age! If she had offered, yes, I would have spent the night with her, I wouldn't lie to you.

"Emily got engaged, a few months ago. You should see the size of him, he's a real muscle-man. He owns a gym. I have a feeling it'll end in tears. All brawn, no brain…"

Elaine looked surprised. Definitely not the sort of man she'd want in her life. Whilst her husband was having amorous thoughts about Emily Brown, she'd been having an affair with her boss, so who was she to pass judgement?

Robbie smiled then squeezed her hand. "Blimey, fancy you remembering all that stuff; still, you've always had a good memory.

"Over the years I've encountered many criminals, some, very dangerous. I'd sort of pushed those two idiots to the back of my mind. It was a lengthy and complicated case, still we had a lot of evidence to pass over to the Thames Valley Police. Oh, yeah, I remember now, asbestos, that's right – from an old market garden in Bexhill, loads of it! They'd dumped it in a country lane, Lower Foxton, not far from here. You know the place, that pretty little village with a derelict windmill."

Elaine nodded. "Umm, I remember you telling me all about it, at the time. Couple o

Irish blokes. They'd fly-tipped a lot of other stuff too, from house clearances. Their faces were on the front page of the Oxford Mail. Good looking blokes too, if they'd been left in the shower for a week! What *was* their surname?

"Now that's something I can't recall!"

Robbie was quiet for a moment. *"Got it!* O'Reilly, yeah, that was it, Patrick and Joseph. What a pair, I wouldn't want to fall out with them. I remember it now – the case revolved around that wealthy guy, Rupert Gilby. He'd employed them to take away all the rubbish, clear the site, but do it on the cheap and as soon as possible. He was well aware there was asbestos on the site. The brothers said, in court, Mr Gilby refused to pay them the going rate. Gilby and his partner, David Fanshawe, wanted to get their garden centre project up and running – asap, they'd big plans for it. Well, back then, East Sussex had nothing like it. They knew the public would go mad for it and the money would come rolling in…

"They all received massive fines, serves 'em right. Going round the countryside, fly-tipping? You know how angry that makes me. Gilby and Fanshawe lied through their teeth. Fancy saying, on oath, they'd never heard of fly-tipping – huh, course they had…"

"Hang on, Rob, I've got a text from Nancy. She's coming over this evening, she's printed off a photo of the orchids, already! Bless her. We've got a nice frame somewhere. Do you remember the painting we bought in the Yorkshire Dales, three sheep in a field? I don't know why we bought it – it's well painted but incredibly boring. I think we wanted something to remind us of the scenery. Those purple orchids will look far better in that frame."

Since being dumped, unceremoniously, by her fiancé, Nancy was spending too much time on her own. She'd begun following the complicated lives of celebrities and the Royal family, her enthusiasm never diminishing.

After hugging both Robbie and Elaine, she put a pile of popular but trashy magazines on the coffee table. Nancy spent a fortune on them, but felt less guilty by passing them on to Elaine. The magazine's editors were happy to print any form of juicy scandal, whether true or false. Nancy had become intrigued by Rupert's disappearance and eager to discuss the whole Gilby family.

Weird and wonderful theories were put forward by members of the public, no matter how ridiculous they sounded. It had even been suggested that Rupert had been abducted by aliens…

After a mug of strong, black coffee, Nancy was in full-flow. "Oh yes, he was kidnapped alright, the police said so. His father paid the ransom, immediately. I heard it was £75,000, I'm not sure if that's the correct figure. No good being too greedy, is it? Still, that Hugo Gilby is a stock-broker, he could afford it – and more!

"Rupert's wife, Roxanne Elliott-Boyd, is convinced he's been murdered by the kidnappers.

"He'd been having an affair with his secretary, Desiree Marlow. Roxy knew what her husband was like – some men just can't keep it in their trousers!"

Robbie's eyes opened wide; surprised that his dear cousin would choose such a crude expression. Nancy continued: "Look, page five, there's a great photograph of Desiree. Beautiful, isn't she? At first, everyone thought they'd run off together, somewhere exotic like the Maldives. Well, they didn't. Desiree has been interviewed by the police, many times. She hasn't a clue where Rupert is. She's been off work, sick with worry. She was madly in love with him, you know. Um, I read that in the Daily Express."

Robbie struggled to get a word in edgeways, so he waited until Nancy was eating a large slice of carrot cake…

"Gilby's disappearance reminds me of Lord Lucan, remember him? He went missing in 1974. Lord Lucan was a merchant banker, just like Rupert, quite a coincidence, eh?

"Some people are convinced, Gilby committed suicide, he felt guilty over the asbestos fiasco. Utter rubbish, of course he didn't. In my humble opinion, the kidnappers have murdered him, that's usually what happens. Once they have the money, they have to kill their victim, he might be able to identify them.

"Rupert had it all, didn't he? Good looks, a new career as an MP, part-owner of Dawson's Garden Centre which is, incidentally, doing very well. I've heard they're opening another branch soon, that'll be the third. Perhaps the kidnappers saw a few photographs of Roxy. I wonder, did that push them over the edge? Well, she's absolutely stunning…

"Rupert's other occupation, as a merchant banker, took him to some classy places. I saw a photograph of him, last year, I believe, in the Financial Times, shaking hands with the French President. Fanshawe and Peabody are financing the renovations of an Art Deco Hotel, right in the centre of Paris. I've heard the loan is for over fifty million pounds – not Euros!"

Elaine looked thoughtful. "D'you think we'll ever know the truth about Lord Lucan's disappearance? Some say he killed himself, yep, jumped off a ferry on his way to France. Others say he had plastic surgery, then his friends whisked him off to South Africa, by boat, where he lived happily for many years. Perhaps Rupert has done something similar. You know what these toffs are like, friends in high places!"

All three laughed. "Oh, aren't we awful?" said Nancy.

Elaine sat on the sofa, admiring the images on Nancy's lap-top. "Oh, look at those poppies, they're lovely. You're a very good photographer, Nancy. D'you know – the poppies remind me of the First World War? Look, Robbie, aren't they beautiful? I wonder why they are only growing in that one place? That's odd. Poppies are usually seen growing in amongst other wild flowers. I can see blue cornflowers, white ox-eye daisies and buttercups; all of them, spread evenly over the field. Look, there's cowslips and red campion too. It's as if Mother Nature puts seeds into a huge bag, shakes them up, them scattered them. The area covered with poppies looks roughly two metres by one metre, that's a bit creepy; one could almost say – the size and shape of a grave."

Elaine stared at her husband. "Robbie, what's wrong? What have I said? You look as white as a sheet!"

"Give me a minute," he replied. He examined his hands, they were shaking. He took a deep breath…

"After the First World War, poppies appeared on battle sites – we all know that. The seeds can lay dormant, buried in the soil, for over a hundred years. However, when the soil is disturbed, *or blown to bits,* as it was in France and Belgium, seeds reach the surface. Once the light, sun and rain have done their job, the seeds can germinate. That's the reason why those *Flanders fields* were suddenly a sea of red."

Elaine didn't want to interrupt her husband, but nevertheless, she did.

"Yes, that makes sense, Robbie, but what are you trying to say?"

Robbie poured himself a glass of Merlot, drinking most of it in one single swig. "The piece of ground in Nancy's photograph has been disturbed, quite recently. I imagine, as it's a *Site of Special Scientific Interest* – and has been so for many years – it will have remained as nature intended, untouched. Besides, the owners of the land are forbidden from digging anywhere in the vicinity. Somehow, the poppy seeds have been churned up and returned to the surface where they've germinated.

"Digging a grave would certainly do such a thing, don't you agree?"

Nancy and Elaine were speechless…

"Nancy, that smallholding you visited in Woodford End, it wasn't owned by an elderly couple, struggling to cope, was it? No, it was owned by two brothers; two very dangerous Irishmen. Do the names Joseph and Patrick O'Reilly mean anything to you?"

Nancy looked shocked, then burst into tears. "Oh my God! Yes, it was their home, their smallholding!

"If only I'd mentioned their surname in my email, you would have warned me – stopped me from going... Honestly, Rob – I was terrified; it was the way they looked at me, as if they intended to rape me. I suggested walking up to the sycamore tree, you know, to check for orchids – well, they became agitated, angry, saying it would be a complete waste of time. They tried to lure me inside, for a cup of tea, I became suspicious. I jumped in my car and drove away as fast as I could. I dare not look back..."

Nancy dabbed her eyes, then took a deep breath; shedding tears had made her feel shaky. Elaine brough over a glass of Merlot, passing it to Nancy.

"Drink this, my love, you're sleeping here tonight, I insist, so there's no need to worry about having a few drinks!"

Nancy recovered her composure. "Robbie, *this grave,* if it is one – are you telling me Rupert's buried there, next to the sycamore tree, underneath a swathe of poppies?"

Robbie shrugged. "Well, he hasn't turned up, has he? The police must have interviewed scores of people, yet no-one's seen him. I'm sure of one thing, the moment Rupert was interviewed by the police – as joint owner of the old market garden site – he would have 'spilt the beans' and provided the brothers names and their mobile number. I bet he didn't take a lot of persuading, either. I remember, in court, when he was under oath, he said he'd no idea where they lived and guess what? I'm sure he was telling the truth. Still, with their criminal record, it wouldn't take long for the police to trace them.

"The O'Reilly brothers should've been given a prison sentence for dumping asbestos – I don't know why they weren't.

"No doubt they hated Rupert, that's why they kidnapped him, plus, of course, the chance of making a tidy sum of money. They'd got his family summed up – yeah, probably looked them up on the internet. His father, a stock-broker? He'd have a very healthy bank account.

"Jealousy is a terrible thing, makes people behave irrationally. As a member of Parliament, Rupert had two jobs and therefore, two huge salaries. Once they'd seen his gorgeous wife and the house at Little Common, I expect they lost the plot, completely! Kidnapping him was like taking candy from a baby. I'm surprised they didn't ask for more than £75,000.

"Right then, guys, first thing tomorrow morning, I'm driving down to Bexhill police station. The chap in charge of the case is a DI, Pete Buxton, I've seen him on the news. Okay, who's coming with me?"

Elaine and Nancy nodded, their faces resembling those of excitable children. Elaine spoke for both of them: "Try stopping us…"

Chapter 31

Loose Ends...

"Sorry to ring you at home, Guv, I had no choice."

"That's alright, Sophie, only I'm not at home, I'm with your mother, we're having a meal at the De La Warr pavilion. We hadn't planned to eat out – it was a spur of the moment thing."

"I'll be two minutes, that's all. For once, you won't mind having your meal interrupted – I promise. I've just taken a call from a Melanie Weston, lives in Hastings, works for Halfords. What she told me will blow your socks off! Right, go ahead and enjoy your meal, then ring me back, soon as you can. *Oh, and both of you – go easy on those delicious puddings!*"

Sophie chuckled, such familiarity! At work he was DI Buxton, Guv, or Sir. At home he insisted, *'Call me Pete.'* It felt odd, as if she were taking liberties. No doubt she'd get used to it. What if he moved in? Could she face him first thing in the morning, nipping out of the bathroom, a fluffy bath towel wrapped around his waist? She scowled: oh my God – even worse – the thought of him, naked and in her mother's bed, oh please, no, that would be *too* embarrassing!

Twenty minutes later, Sophie grabbed her phone, but not before pressing 'mute' on the television. "Hi Sophie, it's me – fire away."

"Okay, sir. Here we go. Not long before Rupert was kidnapped, Melanie Weston was asked to make up a pair of number plates, for a red van. It was the O'Reilly brothers, of course. She wouldn't give me any further info unless I promised to 'look after her.' Her boss must never find out she'd done something wrong, knowingly, and gone against company policy. Yep, you're absolutely right, sir, that's exactly what she did, made the plates without seeing any proof of ownership. Apparently, the customer apologised, saying he'd *left all the paperwork at home.* Bless her, she sounded nervous, but had to admit she'd fallen for Joseph's innate charm, his flattery and his bloody good looks. Sophie tutted.

"The next bit is shocking: it'll send shivers down your spine, I'm not kidding. Joseph bought Melanie a dozen red roses then took her out for a pub meal. Wow, that girl must be desperate – or naïve. After what she described as a 'lovely evening,' Joseph took her back to Bluebell Cottage but soon turned nasty when she refused to go upstairs and have sex with him, there and then, or, wait for it – spend the night in his bed! Can you believe it? He drove her home, in complete silence. I'm happy to say, she's not heard from him since. She's had a lucky escape…

"Anyway, round the back of Bluebell cottage, inside a corrugated iron shed with the door swinging open – Melanie spotted a Royal Mail Van. Guess what? It was displaying the number plates she'd made for them, just the previous week. Why was the van hidden inside a shed? It couldn't be theirs, surely, they're not postmen – it had to be stolen.

"She'd seen you on the national news, sir, on Monday, pointing to a photograph of a red van, asking if anyone was aware of a similar van being stolen.

"After you referred to the murder of that postman, in Hampshire, she knew it was her duty to ring up. She did the right thing by contacting us, but she's worried now, in case she gets the sack for going against company policy. How would she pay the rent?

"I said, don't worry, we won't let anything bad happen to you. DI Buxton will speak to your boss."

"Good work, Sophie. Yes, I'll go and see the boss, no probs. By the way, did you trace the cloned number plate?"

"Oh, yes, I'd forgotten, sorry; so much else going on. I had a word with a few local Royal Mail depots; the number plate cloned by the brothers, matches one of four new vans delivered to the Brighton depot, in early October, 2012.

"Oh, I see," replied Buxton, "They're not as daft as I thought. I wondered if they'd plucked the numbers out of thin air. So, it did come off a genuine Royal Mail van. Worth the effort, I suppose, if they intended to drive around in it. If they were stopped for speeding or got a parking fine, the postman with the genuine number plate would get into trouble! Poor devil…"

"Right then, sir, see you tomorrow. With any luck, we'll tie up a few more loose ends…"

Sophie decided to visit Jenny Dawson, at the garden centre café. If she wanted good advice, or a shoulder to cry on, she could think of no-one better…

"It's good to see you, Sophie, how's work? Oh, silly question. Now the O'Reilly brothers have been arrested, I suppose you're busy preparing the paperwork for their first court appearance, am I right?"

"Yes, you are, Jenny. Piles of paperwork, everywhere. Not everything can be computerized. Even so, it'll be a while yet, six months at least, these things take time. Now listen, everything I tell you is in the strictest confidence, okay?"

Jenny looked over her shoulder, no-one was near enough to hear their conversation. "Yes, of course," she replied, nodding, wisely.

"We have lengthy and compelling witness statements from Nancy Musgrove and Melanie Weston – yep, the O'Reillys must be frightened to death. Rupert's neighbours, George Hanson and Lorraine and Toby Burchell have been amazing, all three have given eye-witness statements. I'm not kidding, they are like gold-dust…

"Both brothers will get a life sentence, there's no alternative for murder *and* for kidnapping. The DI thinks they'll get thirty years. What they did was pure evil. Then it's over to the Hampshire police; Patrick and Joseph will be charged with the murder of that postman. Well, that's gonna be far more difficult to prove; no witnesses. Still, there's always DNA. How did we manage, before it was discovered?

"When they searched Bluebell Cottage, guess what they found in the roof, inside a Jiffy bag? £75,000, the ransom, untouched. The police had marked the fifty-pound notes *and* made a note of the serial numbers. Hugo Gilby wouldn't touch it, he said it was blood money – he'd rather die. *'Give it to charity, please, any one you want.'* It was dreadful, we didn't know what to say.

"Hugo and Alicia have aged, so much, they are hardly recognisable. They've lost their confidence and dare I say, their arrogance. You can see the pain in their eyes."

Jenny looked thoughtful. "To be honest, Sophie, we haven't seen or heard from them since the discovery of Rupert's body, I'm not surprised.

"It's been a difficult time for Danny too. Rupert had been his closest friend, they grew up together, went off to the same university. Sometimes, I don't know what to say to him.

"Poor Roxy, the thought of Rupert's body, lying there in that field – Danny said it's knocked her for six. I think they're feeling guilty because their affair began when Rupert was still alive…"

"That's crazy, and to be honest, quite unnecessary." Sophie looked and sounded angry. "Rupert was carrying on with Desireé Marlow, and by all accounts, she wasn't the

first! He'd taken her to Paris, hadn't he? Yeah, I wonder, *business or pleasure?"*

Jenny stood up. "Give me five minutes, I think we could both do with another latte. Slice of lemon drizzle?"

"Oh, yes please," replied Sophie.

When Jenny returned with the coffees and cake, she remembered Sophie had telephoned her for a reason. "You said on the phone, you wanted to ask me something. A favour, perhaps?"

Sophie smiled, *"Well, yes, in a way..."*

Since giving a detailed statement to the police, Melanie Weston had been suffering from acute anxiety. She was terrified the brothers would seek revenge, even if they were behind bars. They were members of a large, unruly, criminal family, scattered across Southern Ireland, Sussex and Northamptonshire.

They knew where she lived and where she worked. Might her life be in danger?

"Great cake, Jenny. Thanks, I needed that. Right – Melanie is in the process of changing her name, that's a start. She needs a new job and a new beginning. Will you need any more staff at the new garden centre, in St Leonards?"

Jenny winked, then smiled. "Finish your coffee, love, I'll pop in the office and have a few words with Fred."

Ten minutes later, when Sophie saw Fred and Jenny walking towards her, she crossed her fingers, hoping it would be good news.

"No problem," said Fred. "We have a plan. "You've been to our new bungalow, haven't you? It's a big place: four bedrooms plus a smart granny flat with all mod cons! Young Melanie can move into the flat – yes, we'd love that. Since Danny moved in with Roxy, the place is too quiet.

"As for a job, she can pop in and see us, any time, we have plenty of vacancies to fill. Yes, we're hoping to open the new garden centre before Christmas – really looking forward to it…

"Tell Melanie she can move in when she likes, tomorrow, if it suits…"

Sophie stood up and gave them both a hug. "Thanks, Fred, that's brilliant. Thank you both so much, she'll be over the moon. *Just one thing, do you like dogs?"*

Fred and Jenny looked at each other, what an odd question!

"Well, yes, we do," replied Jenny, looking mystified, "although, we haven't had a dog since Danny was a little boy."

Sophie appeared nervous. "Now then, how can I put it? Melanie Weston won't be coming on her own. No. She's been to the RSPCA kennels, in Hastings. Guess what? She took someone home with her, umm, the O'Reilly's dog, *Killer.* Melanie is a sweet girl, she couldn't let that poor, unloved dog spend his remaining days shut away in a dogs' home – even though she knew they'd take great care of him.

"Oh, by the way, as his name doesn't really suit his personality, he has a new, more appealing name – *Kenny,* yes, so much nicer…"

The Dawsons were excited and looking forward to the future. The new garden centre would soon be up and running, and now, right out of the blue, they'd discovered a young lady and a dog who needed to be loved and cared for – by them. It would be an interesting challenge; something to enhance their lives.

Melanie and Kenny would be welcomed with open arms...

Epilogue

"Oh, mum, I can hardly believe it, you and Pete, getting married."

"Well, why not, Sophie? We get on so well. There's a kindly, caring side to him that few people see. As you well know, Pete proposed the moment his divorce came through, so, at our age, why wait?"

A small wedding had been planned, nothing showy, just close friends and family, no more than twenty guests. The reception would be held at the *Jolly Farmer,* a tiny 18th century pub in the pretty village of Upper Banstead.

"Are you sure you'll be able to fit everyone in?" asked Pete, looking concerned.

He'd been reassured by the landlord's confident reply. "Not a problem for us, sir. If necessary, your guests can spill over into our living room. We'd love it!"

Pete had insisted, there must be orchids, *lots of orchids,* no matter what the cost, in fact he'd popped in to have a chat with the local florist. He'd asked her to change Georgia's order, which had been for 'a couple of colourful arrangements' to brighten up the pub. The florist was sworn to secrecy; Pete knew it would be a wonderful surprise for Georgia, his beloved wife to be. The moment she saw the orchids, her face would light up…

Pete smiled, *Georgia Dawn Buxton*. Ah, even better – *Peter and Georgia Buxton;* yes, he liked the sound of it.

When his wife left him, to begin a new life with her sister, in Newcastle, he assumed he'd be single, forevermore…

The ceremony was quite moving, the couple looked so happy together; a few tears were shed by Sophie and a few other ladies. Everything was going according to plan, until the exchange of vows. Pete should have prepared Georgia and Sophie for what was to come and maybe, a few of his close friends too. Why on earth didn't he say something?

Afterwards, at the reception, his cheeks pink (but not through too much champagne). Pete apologised, but that only caused further laughter and teasing…

DI Buxton knew – now that his secret had been announced to the world, there'd be no going back. It wouldn't be long before some smart-arse in Bexhill police station made the most of it! He was dreading it…

"I, Peter Marmaduke Buxton, take thee…" Unsurprisingly, hoots of laughter rang out!

Sophie's eyes opened wide. She looked across at Fred Dawson, his face was a picture. "I don't believe it," he whispered, nearly collapsing with mirth, "blimey, he kept that quiet."

"Stop it, Fred," said his wife, trying to keep a straight face, "behave yourself."

Sitting at the back, newly retired detective sergeant, Sid Byfield, proud Yorkshireman and a man who was known for calling a spade a spade, was overheard saying, rather too loudly, *"Bloody hell, Marmaduke?*

"Fancy giving a child a soppy name like Marmaduke! Makes him sound like a right toff."

Sid and a few other detectives had downed several pints of Newcastle Brown long before two-thirty, the time when the ceremony began. They'd nipped round the corner to the Dog and Duck. Sid laughed, then, looking towards the groom, announced, *"Well, lad, that name has come back to bite thee…"*

A young boy (who'd been told to stop fidgeting and sit still) began shouting at his brother, *"Marmaduke, Marmaduke, your name is Marmaduke!"*

The boy's little brother replied, *"Shut up, I hate you!"* He started sobbing, then kicked his brother quite viciously, in the shins. Their mother, who was looking extremely embarrassed, had to separate them before things got out of hand…

The registrar sighed, then gave up. He may as well stop talking until the wretched sobbing and fits of laughter subsided. Fortunately, he'd been blessed with a good sense of humour. Although rare, this wasn't the first time – and it certainly wouldn't be the last – that 'unusual' names had caused much amusement amongst the guests. "When you are ready," he announced, sounding like a weary headmaster, "perhaps we can continue…"

Pete and Georgia, tired after so much excitement and laughter, were relaxing on the plane, heading for a week's honeymoon in Paris. He kissed her cheek. *"I do love you, Georgia. This has been the best day of my life."*

She squeezed his hand. *"And also, dare I suggest, the most embarrassing?"*

The following morning, when Sophie woke up, she felt a sense of loneliness, the house seemed too quiet. The 'happy couple' had decided to live in Pete's house, she'd just have to get used to it. Nevertheless, she smiled. I bet they're having a wonderful time.

It was during the following afternoon when PC Janice Freeman managed to catch up with Sophie, she'd spotted her, sitting alone in the canteen.

"Ah, DS Hollis, I've been looking for you. Have your ears been burning?"

Sophie smiled, "Um, no more than usual." She pointed towards an empty chair, "Join me."

Janice was feeling uncomfortable. "Huh, now I know how cupid feels."

She continued. "I've just been on a two-day course, *Offender Profiling*. Fascinating: you never know when this sort of stuff might come in handy…

"One of the speakers, Detective Inspector Max Fielding, said he still remembers you: he sends his regards. Apparently, you joined the force on the same day, in Brighton. Is that right?"

Sophie's face lit up. "Oh, my goodness, I am honoured – yes, of course I remember him. Yeah, very good looking, unless he's changed." She giggled.

Janice nodded. "I am *so* glad you said that. DI Fielding asked me to persuade you to go out with him, you know, on a date. He said he'd always fancied you, wow – *you lucky girl!* Would I please put in a good word? Anyway, here's his mobile number. What do you think? Will you be giving him a call?"

What did she think? Well, for a start, thank goodness she was sitting down! Max was the best-looking guy in the force – and an honest man too. Could Max Fielding be the man she'd been searching for, all her life?

Driving home, Sophie struggled to concentrate – if she hadn't been so hungry, she'd have forgotten to stop at the *Happy Plaice,* to pick up some fish and chips…

Sophie's thoughts turned to *Braeside Manor,* she'd loved that book, so full of surprises. She must pass it on to Janice Freeman. You never know – DI Max Fielding might be as desirable as Hamish Alexander Beaufort, the handsome, athletic, charming, wealthy hero of the story.

She looked at herself in the rear-view mirror and chuckled: "Well, I don't care if Max isn't *wealthy,* let's face it – three out of four ain't bad!"

Printed in Great Britain
by Amazon

31315089R00182